Henry Cecil was the pseudonym of Judge Henry Cecil Leon. He was born in Norwood Green Rectory, near London, England in 1902. He studied at Cambridge where he edited an undergraduate magazine and wrote a Footlights May Week production. Called to the bar in 1923, he served with the British Army during the Second World War. While in the Middle East with his battalion he used to entertain the troops with a serial story each evening. This formed the basis of his first book, *Full Circle*. He was appointed a County Court Judge in 1949 and held that position until 1967. The law and the circumstances which surround it were the source of his many novels, plays, and short stories. His books are works of great comic genius with unpredictable twists of plot which highlight the often absurd workings of the English legal system. He died in 1976.

NO FEAR
OR FAVOUR

by

Henry Cecil

HOUSE OF
STRATUS

This edition published in 2000 by House of Stratus, an imprint of Stratus Holdings plc, 24c Old Burlington Street, London, W1X 1RL, UK.

www.houseofstratus.com

Typeset, printed and bound by House of Stratus.

A catalogue record for this book is available from the British Library.

ISBN 1-84232-060-2

Contents

CHAPTER ONE

The Schoolmaster

Hugh Bridges, walking somewhat painfully and very disconsolately in worn clothes and old shoes over hard pavements on a cold December afternoon in London, did not appear to be a fruitful source of blood money to any prospective blackmailer. He was a schoolmaster, fifty-eight years old, kindly and inefficient and of very small means. His wife, whom he adored, was a permanent invalid and his only real happiness in life lay in looking after her. It was when with her that he was able to use the only talent in which he excelled. He was a good reader and nothing gave the couple more pleasure than when they could enjoy together the English classics read by him. He was no actor and no orator and, though he might have obtained a position as an announcer with the BBC (where his abhorrence of the intrusive 'r', so popular with some announcers, would have pleased at least one listener) he never thought of the idea. He had been educated to be a schoolmaster and a schoolmaster he became, good neither at the teaching nor the disciplinary side of his career, but accepted by pupils and colleagues as a friendly member of the staff though one of very small value.

On that December afternoon he was engaged in distributing leaflets advertising washing powder. For some

1

time he had found that he got less and less coaching during the school holidays, for the very good reason that he was an extremely bad coach. But he needed money badly. He wanted to supply his wife with such small luxuries as he could manage to buy, but their rent and rates took a large part of his small salary. He had to find some way of supplementing his income and so he answered an advertisement calling for leaflet distributors. The pay was trifling, thirty shillings for distributing a thousand leaflets, but the few pounds which he could earn meant a lot to them and so he started work. He had to put one leaflet – no more – in the letter box of each house or flat. This often meant climbing up many stairs, and he found that the bundle of leaflets took a very long time indeed to become smaller. As the hours of drudgery went by, hours he could have spent happily with his wife, he wondered how long his present pair of shoes would stand the strain. He was not a strong man, either physically, mentally or morally. He had never done anything plainly wrong because the opportunity had never come his way. But, if he had had the handling of other people's money he would have been sorely tempted to take some for the benefit of his wife, and he would probably have yielded to the temptation. Fortunately he had never had such a temptation to resist.

But on this December afternoon he was suddenly tempted. He was tempted to put more than one leaflet in the same letter box. If found out, he could always say it was an accident. He was careful not to break the rule in houses or flats too near each other. But he soon found that this device did not seem sensibly to lessen the load of leaflets. He thought of his wife sitting waiting at home. And then the Devil, who knows whom and when and where to strike and who presumably decided that he must on this occasion pursue a little man, decided to appear to Hugh Bridges. And he did so in the shape of a dustbin. The Devil is not beautiful, although he can appear in a beautiful disguise. A dustbin does not normally to normal people appear beautiful, but, when the thought occurred to Hugh Bridges, it looked the most beautiful dustbin which he had ever seen. Here was the solution to his troubles. He had enough leaflets left to take up hours of his time. The dustbin smiled at him. 'Come unto me, all ye that are heavy laden ...', it began. That was a false move on the part of the Devil and he immediately regretted it. Hugh Bridges was not a particularly religious man but the words which were put into his mind, though devilishly apt, made him falter in his resolution, when he remembered who had really said them. But by this time the Devil had recovered. The washing powder was no better than anyone else's, thought Hugh. 'He that is without sin among you ...', quoted the dustbin. I don't pretend to be better than anyone else, thought Hugh. I want to be back with my wife, reading to her. It's one of her greatest pleasures, and she gets few enough. The dustbin (with Hugh's assistance) opened its mouth and Hugh, after first looking round to see that he was unobserved, dropped in the remaining leaflets. He hurried home.

The next morning he called at his employers' office and signed the declaration that he had duly distributed all the leaflets in accordance with his instructions and received his money and another bundle of leaflets.

'I was expecting you last night,' said the woman who paid him. 'They took longer than you expected, did they?'

'Er – yes,' said Hugh. 'As a matter of fact it would be a bit easier if I called in for my money next day.'

'That's all right,' said the woman. 'But you're sticking to the rules, aren't you? Only one in each letter box?'

'Oh, of course,' lied Hugh.

Those engaged in distributing agencies of this kind are well aware of the temptations which confront the distributors. And, as far as they can, they take steps to see that their employees do not succumb to these temptations. They employ supervisors, whose business it is to check the movements of distributors. And, once their suspicions are aroused about any particular person, they have him or her watched. The agencies are responsible to the firms who make contracts with them and they would soon lose their business if the leaflets were not, on the whole, distributed properly.

It was not long before the Devil was able to devote his attention to someone else, as Hugh quickly got into the habit of distributing about ten per cent of the leaflets and dumping the rest in various dustbins over his route. His arrangement to call for his money the next day was in case he called back so soon on the day of distribution as to excite suspicion. His behaviour would have been discovered in any case, as the agency which employed him was far more efficient at its job than he was as a schoolmaster. But he did have rather bad luck. He put three leaflets into the letter box of one of the directors of the company which made the soapflakes. The company complained to the agency, the agency had Hugh watched, he was summoned to the office and instantly dismissed. He went home sadly and without his money for that day, though he was not required to repay the money which he had previously received. Now he had to look for some other means of supplementing his income. But, before he had found other employment, he received a call from a man who said his name was Bates.

4

'Yes, Mr Bates,' asked Hugh, 'what can I do for you?'

'You're a master at St Augusta's, Sefton, are you not?'

'I am.'

'I've been sent by the Board of Governors of your school to interview you.'

'Not about retirement, I hope. I'm only fifty-eight.'

'Not specifically about retirement, although that might be involved.'

'But why?' asked Hugh. 'I've had no complaints about my work.'

'Oh no,' said the man, who knew nothing of Hugh's work at the school. 'As far as I know, your work is entirely satisfactory.'

'I'm glad to hear it,' said Hugh.

'When I say that, I'm referring to your work at the school, of course.'

'Quite.'

'But you have been doing some other work, haven't you, at which you were not quite so satisfactory?'

'Other work?' queried Hugh, but he knew what the man meant.

'Distributing leaflets.'

'Yes, I did distribute leaflets for a time.'

'Not very many, I'm afraid,' said the man, 'unless you count dumping them in dustbins proper distribution.'

Hugh said nothing.

'Well,' persisted the man, 'do you call dumping leaflets in dustbins proper distribution?'

'No, I don't.'

'But that's what you did.'

'I'm afraid so. My wife is an invalid and I was desperately tired. I yielded to temptation.'

'D'you mean this only happened once – the time you were caught?'

Hugh did not answer.

'Well, do you?'

'What right have you to ask me these questions?'

'Have you told your headmaster about this?'

'No, I haven't.'

'Don't you think that he and the Governors of the School have a right to know about it?'

'Surely,' said Hugh, 'what I do in my own time is my own affair.'

'Within limits, certainly. But were you not paid for this work?'

'I was.'

'Did you not sign a declaration that you'd done the work properly before you were paid?'

'Yes, I did.'

'You were paid on the strength of that declaration.'

'I suppose so.'

'But the declaration wasn't true. You hadn't distributed all the leaflets properly. You'd put most of them in dustbins.'

'Not for the first few times.'

'But certainly for the last few times.'

'I'm afraid so.'

'So you obtained money by telling a lie.'

'If you put it like that, yes.'

'How would you put it?'

'I don't know,' said Hugh unhappily.

'Getting money by telling a lie is called fraud,' said the man. 'People can be prosecuted for it.'

'The agency knows all about it.'

'That's, of course, why they dismissed you?'

'Yes.'

'But they haven't prosecuted you – so far.'

'No.'

'They could, couldn't they?'

'They never suggested that they would.'

'Well, if you're lucky, they won't, but don't you think the authorities of your school ought to be told about serious crimes you commit in the holidays?'

'I've never thought about it.'

'Well, think about it now,' said the man. 'You are partly responsible for the boys' moral welfare. Is it desirable that a person who can be prosecuted for fraud should teach children? He might teach them how to do the same thing.'

'Oh, I wouldn't dream of it.'

'It may be you would and it may be you wouldn't,' said the man. 'But isn't that a matter for your headmaster or the Board of Governors to judge?'

'I don't know.'

'At any rate, you haven't told them?'

'No – but as they've sent you, I suppose they know. I wonder how.'

'Mr Bridges, have you ever been guilty of any similar conduct?'

'Never,' said Hugh. 'Upon my honour, never.'

'The honour of a man who tells lies to get money isn't worth all that much, is it?'

'No, I suppose not.'

'But it's true, is it? You've led a blameless life until this episode?'

'It's absolutely true.'

'I must think,' said the man. He waited for about a minute. During the first half of it he looked steadily at a wall of the room, during the second he rose and paced up and down. Finally he spoke.

'I've got some good news for you, Mr Bridges,' he said. 'I'm not from the Governors of your school after all.'

'But – ' began Hugh.

'Wait a moment, please. I'll explain. I come from a body called the Association for the Protection of the Public from Fraud. One of our methods is to give people who are guilty of fraud but not prosecuted a nasty fright. This should ensure that they don't do it again.'

'Well, you've certainly given me a fright,' said Hugh. 'But, even if you hadn't, I should never have done it again. I was heartily ashamed of myself.'

'Only after you were caught,' said the man. 'If you hadn't been caught, you'd have been collecting your money for dumping leaflets in dustbins up to this moment. Indeed, at this particular time you might have been dumping a load.'

'No,' said Hugh with a faint smile. 'I should have been home by now. One of the reasons I did it was to get back to my invalid wife.'

'Well, I'm glad to hear it,' said the man. 'That may enable my executive to take a lenient view. No promises, mind you.'

'How d'you mean, a lenient view?'

'Well – you don't suppose I've come all this way for nothing, do you? The Association pays me, and it expects to get results.'

'But I thought you'd come to give me a fright.'

'That was one object certainly,' said the man. 'I'm glad to think it may have been effective.'

'Oh, it has been, I assure you.'

'Good. Now comes the next question.'

He paused in order to give Hugh a chance to wonder what the next question was.

'No doubt you'd like to know what it is,' he said.

'Yes, I would,' said Hugh.

'Then I'll tell you. The question is – should the Association report the matter to your headmaster?'

'I see.'

'To report or not to report, that is the question. D'you think we should?'

'Well, naturally I don't. I might lose my job.'

'You think they might sack you, do you?'

'I suppose it's possible.'

'Well, Mr Bridges, if it's as serious as all that, I should have thought it was plainly your duty to tell them yourself.'

'If I lost my job, I don't know what would become of us.'

'If you'd been sent to prison, what would have become of you? You'd certainly have lost your job then, wouldn't you?'

'Yes, I suppose so.'

'You know, the trouble is, Mr Bridges, that an Association like ours does a tremendous amount of work entirely for the public good but no one thanks us. I don't suppose you've ever seen our name in the Press.'

'I can't say that I have.'

'If we didn't get support from voluntary subscriptions, we'd have to close down. Fortunately there are just enough public-spirited people about to keep us going. But they die or go abroad or take up some other charity and we need new blood the whole time. They have to pay me a decent salary or I wouldn't do the work. It's not work you can give to anyone. You've got to have someone with – well – I don't want to boast – with – what shall we say? – more than average intelligence. So they get chaps like me, who otherwise would be making a lot of money in commerce. But it all has to be paid for.'

He stopped and then added: 'You wouldn't like to become a subscriber, I suppose,' he said.

'We can hardly get through as it is,' said Hugh.

'If you lose your job, you won't get through at all.'

'That's true,' said Hugh.

'You see,' said the man, 'my people have got to weigh your case up against the others. I'm not pretending there are not many worse cases than yours, and if I were able to report that you were prepared to become a subscriber, they might think that would sufficiently show your good faith and justify them in not reporting the matter to your headmaster.'

'I see,' said Hugh. 'Well, I suppose I might manage a couple of guineas a year, if that would help.'

'It would not,' said the man. 'I'm afraid I've been wasting your time and mine. I'm so sorry.'

He got up to go.

'But what will happen?' asked Hugh anxiously.

'I'm afraid that I shall be instructed by my executive to tell your headmaster all about it.'

'Please don't,' said Hugh.

'It's not in my hands. I'm only an agent. I only report what's happened.'

'If you could report that I'd subscribe a bit more, would it help?

'Of course it would. Your money would help us to catch far worse criminals than you. What's your salary?'

'Nine fifty after tax.'

'Net, that is?'

'Yes.'

'Humph! Suppose we say twenty per cent.'

'Twenty per cent!!' said Hugh in horrified tones.

'Per annum,' said the man.

'Every year!!'

'You can pay by the week. Say four pounds a week.'

'I can't possibly afford it.'

'I quite understand,' said the man, and grasped the door handle. 'Thank you for seeing me and being so frank about everything.'

'Wait a moment,' said Hugh. 'If I made it three, would that do?'

'Three pounds a week?'

'Yes,' said Hugh. 'Though I really don't know how I can do even that.'

'That's quite simple,' said the man. 'We're not like a hire-purchase company. We don't have signed agreements. We're not like the ordinary charity. We don't even want seven-year covenants. When you feel you can't pay, you just stop paying. As I said, you don't even have to start paying.'

'But, if I don't, you'll go to the school.'

'Of course. We have our duty to do.'

'And if I stop paying – that's what'll happen?'

'Quite right. Every Friday at the corner of Wharton Street, a man called Smith will collect the money from you.'

'But when I'm at school?'

'Of course. How silly of me. You can send it by post to this address.'

He handed Hugh a piece of paper with an address on it. 'You can do that from the start, as a matter of fact. Every Friday three pounds to this address. But you don't have to start or keep it up, if you don't want to. Please feel absolutely free to do just as you please. Now I really must be going. I've got a much worse case than yours to attend to. We wouldn't *let* a man like him subscribe to our Association. His money would contaminate us. No, we'll get him a nice long stretch instead. Goodbye, Mr Bridges. Thank you for being so co-operative.'

CHAPTER TWO

An Attractive Girl

'The wilderness and the solitary place shall be glad for them,' read Mr Slaughter, 'and the desert shall rejoice, and blossom as the rose.'

The congregation sat back to listen. Mr Slaughter not only had an extremely pleasant voice but, like Mr Bridges, he knew how to read. It was about the only quality which the two men had in common but it was certainly not due to this fact that Mr Slaughter also attracted the attentions of a blackmailer. He was, on the face of it, a much more promising subject for blackmail. He had ample means, he was a family man with a wife and children to whom he was devoted, and he liked going to church. The congregation enjoyed listening to him almost as much as he enjoyed reading to them. He looked at them as he read and did not, as do most readers of the Lessons, keep his eyes glued to the Bible.

But, if you are going to read the Lessons regularly (whether you look at the congregation as you read or not), and if you are well-to-do and a good family man, you must be careful what you do outside the family and outside your church. Because, as Mr Slaughter found, you are vulnerable if you do things which you shouldn't do. As Mr Slaughter left the church that morning with his wife and elder son he noticed an attractive young woman of about thirty on the other side of the road. She did not smile at him but she returned his gaze in a not unfriendly manner.

'Yes, she's very pretty,' said his wife. 'I don't blame you.' But she would have blamed him very much if he had done more than look.

At about 7.30 p.m. on the following Thursday the same young woman was standing in a street in Soho not far from a strip-tease club. She was watching the entrance. Ten minutes later, with his hat pulled down as far as possible over his head and wearing dark glasses, Mr Slaughter emerged. He was followed by a girl. They talked together for a few minutes and she gave him a piece of paper. Then he went off towards a car park, removing his hat and his dark glasses as he went. He was totally unaware that he had been observed.

About a week later as he walked from his car to his office, the young woman, to whom his wife had referred near their church, approached him.

'Excuse me,' she said. 'Didn't we meet outside church at Longton?'

He remembered her face, and knew they hadn't met. But Cornhill was a long way from St Peter's Church and from his home. He was pleased too that the young woman obviously must have liked the look of him. After all he was nearly twice her age.

'Of course,' he said. 'Would you lunch with me?'

'I'd love it.'

They fixed a time and place and duly met.

After the usual opening conversation he said: 'I'm very flattered that you wanted to see me again.'

'I don't think your wife would approve.'

'Oh, I don't know,' he said uncomfortably.

'She's very jealous, isn't she?'

'How on earth d'you know?'

'A woman knows these things,' said the girl. 'I could tell by the way she looked – or rather didn't look at me outside church.'

'Well,' he conceded, 'it's different with women. They're monogamous. We're polygamous. I think the Victorians had the right idea. A man could do what he liked outside his home, so long as he didn't bring the other ladies to the house. A few did but they were called cads. A man in my position could have his mistresses, and both husband and wife knew it. But nothing was ever said. The decencies – if that is the right word – were duly observed. And everyone was happy. A bit hard on the wives, I suppose, but that's nature.'

'It's much harder for men like you today.'

'Much harder?' he said. 'What do you mean?'

'Well – you are a polygamist. It's harder for you to have your other wives and keep your present one.'

'That's absolutely true,' he said. 'If you and I are going to see more of each other, I'll have to be extremely careful.'

'Do you want to see more of me?' she asked.

'Very much so.'

He had never been approached in this way by any girl who wasn't a tart. This was a new and very pleasant experience. I suppose, he said to himself, she's a nymphomaniac, but why should she be attracted to me? It really is rather gratifying. He straightened his tie.

'You're a very attractive girl,' he said.

'Thank you. I must say I was amazed when I found out how old you were.'

'How old am I?'

'You're fifty-six next birthday.'

'How on earth d'you know?'

'When I'm interested in anyone I like to know as much as I can about them.'

'But how did you find out? Did you see the vicar or someone?'

'No – I went to the fountain head. I turned you up in Somerset House.'

For the first time since the girl had approached him Mr Slaughter regretted it. He suddenly had a cold feeling in the pit of his stomach. Somerset House! Why on earth was a stranger looking up his birth certificate?

'That's an odd thing to do,' he said as nonchalantly as possible.

'It is rather. But then the whole thing's rather odd, isn't it? Do you usually pick up girls in the City?'

'You picked me up.'

'True enough. That's odder still. Have you ever in your life before been picked up in the City by – I hope I may call myself – a respectable-looking girl?'

'No, I certainly haven't. Or by any other girl either.'

'Not in the City perhaps.'

'What on earth d'you mean by that?'

'Only what I said. That you hadn't been picked up by any girl *in the City*.'

She underlined the last three words.

There was a short silence.

'I don't think after all,' he said, 'that I want our short association to continue.'

'That's a pity,' said the girl, 'because it's going to.'

'What on earth d'you mean by that?'

'No more than I said. And no less. I wish our association to continue.'

'That may be,' he said, 'and I confess I can't think why you do. But without meaning to be offensive, I'm afraid I want it to end. Now.'

15

'I dare say you do,' said the girl with biting sweetness. 'But you can't always have your own way.'

'In a few minutes I shall pay the bill, and then I'm afraid we shall go our respective ways.'

'No doubt,' said the girl, 'but we shall meet again. And often. Or at any rate as often as is necessary.'

'Why have you been going into my affairs?'

'What makes you think I have?'

'Don't be silly. You've been to Somerset House. You know about local affairs although I don't think you live in the neighbourhood. This is all part of a plan.'

'Well,' said the girl, 'you're perfectly right. It is. Shall I tell you?'

'You'd better.'

'I detect a threatening note,' said the girl. 'Are you threatening me?'

'It's the other way round.'

'Is it? What have I threatened you with?'

'You're leading up to it.'

'You asked me to go on. Would you prefer me to stop?'

'I warn you. I am not easily frightened and I won't be trifled with,' said Mr Slaughter.

'Well, that's a lie to begin with. You're frightened as hell. When I mentioned Somerset House you went white. That's a thing one can't control.'

'What do you want?'

'Nothing at this precise moment.'

'What is this plan?'

'So you really want to know. All right then, as you're not to be trifled with and you've asked me, I'll tell you. Ready?'

'Go on,' he said.

'I come from an old-fashioned group of which you won't have heard. It calls itself the Institute for Cleaner

Morals. Like to join? Then I could send you all our literature.'

She stopped.

'Well,' she went on, 'like to join?'

He felt compelled to say something.

'What is it?'

'Its name explains it. I'm just an employee. We're run by a group of people who are greatly disturbed by the present moral laxity among all sections of the population. Not just among teenagers – but equally among people of your age. They believe that, unless a strong line is taken by someone, this moral degeneration will continue with the inevitable result that this country will go completely to the dogs. They say it's only half way there at the moment and they want to stop the impetus and to try to get an impetus the other way. It's uphill work, as you can imagine. No government will help. Indeed the tendency of modern legislation is to make it easier to be immoral, not more difficult. The Church seems powerless, though no doubt it does its best. So a band of men and women have got together to try to stem the tide. You approve, I hope?'

'In principle, yes,' he said.

'I'm glad to hear you say that,' said the girl. 'But didn't the words stick in your throat a bit?'

'I don't know what you mean.'

'Oh yes, you do. And perfectly well. But, as you say you don't, I'll have to be more explicit. You've already been pretty frank to me about your views on your marriage vows.'

'I've said nothing about my marriage vows.'

'Oh yes, you have. All this talk about polygamy and monogamy. You said that when you thought you were going to have a nice little affair with me.'

17

'I see,' he said. 'So your object was to see if I could be tempted?'

'No,' she said. 'It wasn't. I know you can be and have been. So there was nothing new to find out.'

'What is it, then?'

'My Institute thinks it's a bad thing for a leader of the people, and in your own small way – in local affairs – you are one, to preach one thing and practise another.'

'I don't preach.'

'Everyone who accepts certain responsibilities preaches. You can't become a churchwarden without saying implicitly that – what shall we say? – adultery, for example, is a bad thing. You can't read the Lessons regularly in church without implicitly saying that you stand in a general sense for what the Church stands for. And I have yet to learn that the Church stands for sleazy strip-tease clubs and for assignations with prostitutes.'

Mr Slaughter went white again. He realised that he had been followed and watched, but to what extent and why he did not know.

'I've asked you before, what do you want? What *do* you want?'

'To make you a disciple. To convert you. Instead of Mr Slaughter joining in the general moral degeneracy, to have him with us helping to set the country on the right road again.'

'You simply want me to join your Institute?'

'Exactly.'

'And if I don't?'

'If you don't, you don't.'

'And what will happen, if I don't?'

'We shall have to try other methods of effecting your cure.'

'Why have *I* been selected?'

'Oh don't think you're the only one. Not by any means. If you *were* the only one, there'd be no need for the Institute.'

'How do I join – *if* I do?'

'You just tell me you will. We don't believe in signatures and written undertakings to abide by all sorts of rules. You simply tell me you wish to join and that you subscribe to our principles.'

She slightly underlined the word 'subscribe'.

'And that's positively all.'

'Positively all,' she said. 'Of course,' she added, 'if you like to support the movement in a practical way we shall be only too delighted. We subsist on voluntary subscriptions. But don't get the idea that you have to subscribe – or that if you do, you have to continue. You don't have to start, and, if you start, you don't have to go on.'

'And if I do nothing?'

'I shall simply report the matter to those who sent me.'

'And what will they do?'

'That's for them to decide.'

'But you must know the sort of thing they'd do. You talked about other methods of effecting a cure.'

'Well, some ailments need a doctor. The patient can't cure himself. He doesn't know enough. But you know perfectly well what you're suffering from. So you know what to do. The first thing would be to inform your wife and the vicar how you've been behaving and to promise to behave yourself in the future.'

'I see,' he said. 'So, if I don't subscribe to your Institute, you or one of your colleagues will tell my wife and the vicar what you've found out about me.'

'I never said any such thing,' said the girl. 'I merely told you what *you* ought to do. You don't *have* to do it. You don't have to subscribe. You don't have to do anything at all, except tell me to go away, and go home to your wife and read the Lessons next Sunday.'

'What sort of subscription would be acceptable?'

'If you really want to help the movement and at the same time to show your contrition you should obviously give a substantial amount. I wouldn't dream of saying that if you weren't a pretty wealthy man. I mean, it's like fines in court. £500 would mean nothing to you. It would break a smaller man.'

'£500 would mean a lot to me.'

'But it certainly wouldn't break you – or even interfere with your standard of living. You'd simply have to sell a small part of some investment. That's true, isn't it?'

'No, it wouldn't break me.'

'But it wouldn't interfere with your standard of living, would it?'

'I suppose not.'

'If a burglar stole it and you weren't insured, it would just be a very considerable annoyance?'

'Well?'

'Well, this should give you pleasure, not annoy you. You'll be helping a great and valuable movement.'

'And you think I should pay £500?'

'It doesn't matter what I think.'

'But it does. Do you consider £500 the right sum?'

'Well, as you ask me, I don't. You ought to give something that hurts. £500 would annoy but not hurt. Now suppose you gave, say, £2,000 and £500 a year, that might hurt a bit, and you could really feel that you were redeeming your lost soul.'

'£2,000 and £500 a year!! This is monstrous,' he said. 'I shall go to the police.'

'By all means,' said the girl. 'And I shall go back to my Institute – *and* to our solicitors.'

She started to tidy herself for leaving.

'I told you from the beginning that there was no need for you to subscribe anything. And, when you go to the police, tell them that they can have a complete recording of this interview. I keep a little thing in my handbag. It prevents mistakes and misunderstandings afterwards. Goodbye.'

She got up.

'Wait a moment,' he said. 'Perhaps I was too hasty.'

'There's no perhaps about it. You were. Goodbye.'

'No, please don't go for a moment. Sit down. Please.'

'Oh, very well, just for a moment. Why?'

'I'd like to subscribe to your Institute.'

'I don't think we want a subscription from anyone who talks about the police.'

'I'm sorry. I shouldn't have said that. You'd like it in cash, I suppose?'

'£2,000 in cash? I should think not. What d'you think we are? Bank robbers?'

'You mean I can send a cheque?'

'Of course you can. What else? You don't seem to realise who you're dealing with. Of course your money can be traced. Did you really think I wanted two thousand dirty one pound notes? Now I really must be going. If you want to subscribe here's the name and address. All cheques should be made out to the Institute and not to an individual. I look forward to hearing you read the Lessons again. In church, I mean, not outside the Tingle-Tingle Club.'

CHAPTER THREE

The Bank Clerk

Richard Allen was on the way up in the banking world. At the early age of thirty-two he had become a branch accountant and with luck he would become a manager before he was much, if at all, past forty. As soon as he had received his last increase of salary he had married a girl whom he had loved and who had loved him for three years. He had refused to marry until he considered his income justified it. They had two small children. Everything seemed set fair.

Like all but the tiny percentage of bank clerks who are tempted by the money which goes through their hands, Richard was a person of integrity. He enjoyed his work and he loved his wife and children. And then misfortune came. He backed the winner of the Derby and made £25. It is a strict rule of banks that their employees may not gamble and any clerk who was found to be a gambler would risk instant dismissal. Most people can gamble and lose without resorting to crime. But there are some who can't. The temptation to a cashier to 'borrow' money to put on a certain winner in order to recover somewhat heavy losses is sometimes too great. There must have been some who did it with success. Who took the plunge, 'borrowed' the money, won, repaid it without being discovered and never gambled again. The torture such people suffer while waiting for the result of the race and wondering whether, even if the horse won, they would be found out, is fortunately too much for some of them. They thank Heaven and sin no more.

But others are not so lucky. And once they start on the downward path their eventual doom is usually certain. Modern taxation has certainly encouraged gambling to a very great extent. It is the only honest way in which a person without capital can make a substantial sum without having to pay tax on it. But this method of increasing his income is denied to the bank clerk.

Richard had never been tempted to gamble before. His occasional bet on the National or the Derby was not so much a gamble as falling into line with the rest of the world.

'Shall I put a £1 on for you, old man?' asked his neighbour. 'It's going to spring a big surprise.'

'OK,' said Richard and thought no more about it, until he was delighted to receive £25 for his £1. He spent all the money on his wife. It made them both very happy. It was a new experience and a very pleasant one. Why not repeat it? He did and won again – unfortunately. This time it was only £5. But it was enough to buy a new scarf for his wife. He knew, of course, that it was against the rules of the bank, but there was nothing illegal or dishonest about it. Moreover there were so many betting shops that there was no question of having to open an account with a bookmaker. If it had been in the days when betting could only be conducted by having an account with a bookmaker or by illegal street betting, Richard would never have succumbed or been tempted to do so. But betting shops have made it easy for everyone. Have a quick look round to see if there's anyone you know about, pull your hat down as far as possible, walk in quickly, place your bet and out you go and no one any the wiser.

Richard started to back horses regularly and sensibly. He never plunged heavily and, had he been left alone, he would never have been in the least tempted to use the bank's money for his purposes. He won a little, lost a little, lost a little again, won a little and on the whole was a little down over the year. But, of course, the fun was forgetting his losses and buying something with his winnings. So, though he knew that he must have made an overall loss, he found the pleasure of winning more than made up for it. And, provided he always bets well within his means, the average punter enjoys himself and comes to no harm. Richard would have come to no harm at all, if he had not been employed in a bank.

One day, when he was sitting at lunch in a restaurant, the man opposite him spoke.

'That was a nice win you had on Bosun's Mate,' he said.

'What did you say?' said Richard.

The man repeated what he had said.

'How d'you know about it?'

'I was told.'

'Who by?'

'Does it matter? It isn't a crime, is it?'

'What has it to do with you?' asked Richard.

'Don't take offence, old man,' said the stranger. 'I just wanted to be sure it was you. So long.'

And he left.

Richard was puzzled but not unduly worried until, a few days later, as he was walking towards the station on his way home, another stranger accosted him.

'Excuse me, might I have a word with you? You are Mr Richard Allen?'

'Yes, I am.'

'I'd just like a word if I may.'

'May I ask who you are and what it's about? I don't think I know you.'

'No, you don't. Could you perhaps spare me five minutes?'

'Not unless you tell me what it's about.'

'I'd rather do that where it's a bit quieter.'

'You can either tell me now or not at all.'

'Oh, very well,' said the man. 'I'm only thinking of your interests. I'm employed by the Bankers' Protection Association.'

'What's that?' asked Richard.

'It's what it says. It's an association for the protection of bankers.'

'I've never heard of it.'

'Well, you have now. But, if you'd rather not discuss the matter with me, I can easily go to your manager instead.'

'What matter?' asked Richard.

'You know well enough,' said the man. 'Why beat about the bush?'

'What matter?' repeated Richard.

'Look, Mr Allen, I'm a busy man. I've got a lot of other people to see. If you'd prefer me to discuss it with your manager, just say so and I won't trouble you a moment longer.'

Richard hesitated. There was only one matter which he would not want the man to discuss with his manager and he felt sure that this was it. He now remembered the other stranger, who had mentioned his bet on Bosun's Mate.

'Very well,' he said. 'I'll have a chat with you, but I haven't much time.'

'Nor have I,' said the man. 'Let's go through here. There's an empty seat in that churchyard. I like to be able to look at a person when I'm talking to him and you can't when you're walking.'

They walked in silence to the seat and sat down. 'Well, now,' said the man. 'It's bad, isn't it? A young man like you well on the road to success. Why d'you do it?'

'Do what?' persisted Richard.

The man got up.

'I can't waste any more of my time,' he said. 'I'll go to your manager.'

Richard gave in.

'You mean I've been backing horses?' he said.

'Well, I'm not aware of anything else. But, if you've been pinching cash as well, you'd better say so at once. You'll lose your job, of course, but it'll pay off in the long run.'

'Of course I haven't taken a thing,' said Richard indignantly.

'No need to be so angry,' said the man. 'One thing leads to another, and you must well know that gambling by employees is forbidden by banks in case they try to make up their losses out of the till. You signed an undertaking not to gamble when you joined the bank, didn't you?'

'What do you want?' asked Richard.

'Just to have a chat. Now you've never heard of the Bankers' Protection Association. BPA, for short. Perhaps you're surprised that bankers need protection as much as anyone else. D'you know how much is lost to the banks by fraudulent employees?'

'No, I don't, as a matter of fact.'

'Well, it's confidential, or I'd tell you. But it's the deuce of a lot. The only thing to do is to try to stop it at the source. You may not be surprised to learn that nine-tenths of the chaps who steal have been driven to it, as they call it, by gambling. Of course they're not *driven* to it at all. If they'd any guts, they'd make a clean breast of it and start

26

afresh. But they haven't any guts. So they take what seems to them the easy way out. And that's the end. Now there's nothing new about that. That's as old as the banks themselves. But there *is* a very serious problem today. As you must know, there's a great shortage of young men coming into the banks. Young men of the right standard, I mean. And, if the banks dismissed every employee who ever had a bet, they'd be thinner on the ground than ever. So that's where the BPA comes in. If your manager knows you're a gambler, you're out. He's probably no alternative but to sack you. If only for the sake of example. But provided you haven't been dipping your hand in the till, the banks would like to keep you if they could do so safely. That is, without your doing it again and without a bad example being set. So the BPA keeps its eye on you. Not on everyone, of course, but on a fair number. It makes enquiries. It has its sources of information. You won't be surprised to learn that bookies' offices yield a great deal of it. Then, when we've discovered a culprit, a BPA agent gets in touch with him. In the first instance the manager knows nothing. If all goes well, he doesn't need to know. Of course, if the suspect is difficult, the BPA just hands the matter over to the man's manager and goes out of the picture. Now the first question I have to ask you, Mr Allen, is do you wish the BPA to stay in the picture or go out of it?'

Richard did not answer at first.

Then he said: 'I just don't know what to say.'

'It's taken the stuffing out of you, hasn't it? A young married man with two kids, well on the way to success, and bang! he's out on his ear.'

'You know all about me, then?'

'We know enough to know that you are worth helping.'

'How can you help me?'

27

'Oh, that's quite simple. But first of all I've got to know if you want us to deal with the matter or if it's to go through your manager.'

'Naturally I don't want to lose my job.'

'Then you'd like us to deal with the matter?'

'Yes, please,' said Richard.

'Right,' said the man. 'Now we can talk. Now, first of all, you must promise not to mention this conversation to any living soul. Before you promise, I'll tell you the reason. It's very important that the BPA should be as secret as possible. If it were well known, it would have to give up. The Press would get on to it – "Bankers' Secret Association" and all that. It would have to be scrapped. That will happen one day. There's bound to be a leak. But, until that time comes, we go on doing our work. And very useful work it is. D'you know that this year we've saved nearly a hundred and fifty clerks who'd otherwise have been lost to the banks? That's quite a few. And human material is about all this country has left. So, first of all, have I your promise?'

'Yes,' said Richard.

'Good,' said the man. 'Secondly, of course, I must have your word of honour that never as long as you're employed by the bank will you enter into any form of gambling whatever – no horses, no pools, no casinos, nothing.'

'I promise,' said Richard.

'It's an easy enough promise to make, but you've got to keep it. Not even a bit on the Derby. You understand that. No exceptions whatever.'

'I understand,' said Richard. 'I will never in any circumstances gamble again.'

'That's fine,' said the man, 'if you keep to it. And, don't forget, this may help you, we know you now and we'll check up every now and then. That may encourage you to keep your promise.'

'I'd keep it anyway,' said Richard.

'That's how you feel now,' said the man. 'It'd be strange if you didn't, when you can see your whole life flying out of the window unless you do promise. Well, that's that, then.'

The man got up.

'Is that all?' said Richard.

The man sat down again.

'I must be slipping,' he said. 'Yes, those are the most important things. But my people want some kind of a guarantee you'll keep your promise.'

'But then I'd have to tell someone about it.'

'No, we don't want a personal guarantor. Your own surety will be enough.'

'My own surety?'

'That's right. You'll get it back in the end.'

'Get what back?'

'The deposit or whatever you like to call it.'

'Deposit?'

'Yes, an annual deposit. My people take the view that if you put down, say, three or four hundred a year for, say, five years you'll have an incentive to keep your word. Actually it's a form of compulsory saving. You get five per cent interest on your money.'

'You mean I'm to pay three or four hundred a year for five years?' said Richard.

'D'you think it's too much?'

'It is.'

'Then it'll make you remember all the more, won't it? And it'll be quite a little nest egg at the end, won't it? Let's say £250. You'll have £1,250 plus interest to come back at the end. There's your deposit for a house, if you haven't already got one.'

'What'll happen if I don't pay?'

'Nothing,' said the man. 'Nothing at all. It's a purely voluntary payment to guarantee your good faith. If you don't want to pay it or can't afford to do so, don't. That's quite all right.'

'What would I gain by paying it?'

'Well, first of all it would be a very good way of reminding you to keep your word, and it would keep you a bit short of money for luxuries like horse-racing. Secondly, as I said, it's an excellent form of saving – thirdly it means that the BPA will take your word. They've never yet been let down by a man who's given security.'

'And what about people who haven't given security?'

'The trouble with them is that they need watching. And, of course, mistakes do occur.'

'Mistakes? What sort of mistakes?'

'Well, as I told you, a man doesn't get a second chance. If you have another bet after this, your manager will be told at once.'

He paused for so long that Richard had to ask a question.

'I see that, but where does the mistake come in?'

'Oh – the mistake,' said the man, 'the mistake. Well, you see, if a man hasn't given security he might keep his word and he might not. In either case he might be reported to his manager. If he hadn't kept his word, he'd deserve it, but, if he had, it would be a mistake.'

'So you mean, even if I did keep my word, my manager might still be told about my gambling up to now.'

'Only by mistake,' said the man, 'but people are only human and mistakes do occur. They're quite unavoidable, you know.'

'So the only way to be sure that I don't get wrongly reported to my manager, is to give security.'

'I won't say it's the only way, but it's the best way I know.'

'How am I to pay?'

'Well, you understand that it can't be by cheque or everyone would get to know about it. And I don't expect you to produce £250 in cash. Let's say £20 a month in cash. But, as I've said, you don't have to pay it.'

'Where should I send it?'

'To this address.'

The man handed him a card with 'BPA, 11 Featherston Street, SE7' on it.

'Shall we say on the 1st of each month?' he said. 'But only if you want to. And, if you find it too much, stop it altogether.'

'Wouldn't it be better to send a little less rather than stop it altogether?'

'No,' said the man. 'Send £20 a month or nothing at all. We know your salary and the amount is fixed so that you *can* pay it, even though at times you'll find it a hardship. That's intended. It would be a greater hardship to lose your job, wouldn't it? Now if there's nothing else you'd like to ask, I must go on to my next job. Good evening.'

Richard went home in a very troubled frame of mind. He longed to discuss the matter with his wife, but felt he mustn't. The next morning after he'd been at work for about an hour he was sent for by the manager. His heart sank. Something he'd said must have annoyed the BPA man and he'd reported him just the same. Or perhaps he ought to have offered some payment there and then. He went white and unhappy to the manager's office.

'Hullo, Allen,' said the manager. 'Why, what's the matter? Aren't you well?'

'I'm quite all right, thank you, sir,' said Richard.

'Well, sit down, you don't look it. Have a glass of water. Had a sudden shock or something?'

'This happens occasionally,' said Richard. 'It's nothing. I've been tested for it. Thank you, sir.'

He drank some water.

'Good,' said the manager. 'Well, we'll be sorry to lose you, but – '

Richard had gone very white.

'Have some more water. You're sure you shouldn't see a doctor?'

'Well – you did give me a shock, sir – talking about my leaving like that – I mean – I hope, that is – '

'Sorry,' said the manager. 'Silly of me. You've been happy here no doubt – it's a happy branch – and it's always a jolt to leave – I found it so myself – but you can't afford to miss this chance. They're going to transfer you to a branch at Minton. It's a busy place and, if all goes well, you should be assistant manager there within a couple of years. That's the idea anyway. Not bad, assistant manager at thirty-four. I didn't do anything like as well.'

'That's wonderful news, sir, but I shall hate leaving here. I've enjoyed serving under you so very much.'

'Nice of you to say so. But you'll enjoy people serving under you even more. It's not for a month. So you've got some time to make your arrangements. And there's a flat you can rent if you want it. Don't talk about it until just before you go. There might be a little jealousy. You see, you're pretty young to get the job. But I'm glad to say I was able to recommend you one hundred per cent. You'll get a small increase to start with, but, when you become assistant manager, it rises fairly steeply. Now, how are you feeling?'

Richard was feeling distinctly better, and he had made up his mind on one important subject. Up till that moment he had not been sure whether to pay the BPA or tell them to go to hell and take the consequences. Now he had made up his mind to pay.

CHAPTER FOUR

The Councillor

If everyone who could be sued for slander were in fact sued, the courts would have to deal with more slander actions than accident cases. But few slanders are revealed to the persons slandered. Fortunately. There cannot be many people who do not at some time in some company, whether in a club, a public house or their own home, say something slanderous about a man or a woman, something which the slanderer could not prove to be true and which he did not utter on a privileged occasion. Damages in plenty there would be if the fact of the slander were known. But worse than that friendships would be broken and quite a number of people would have to leave the close community in which they lived. You could not continue to live in a village if it were known that you had falsely accused the postmistress of eavesdropping on the telephone, the postman of stealing registered letters, one farmer of making fraudulent returns and another of poaching his neighbour's pheasants. Even if each allegation were in fact true. Unless you could prove it to be true it might just as well be false.

There indeed is an untapped field for the blackmailer. In a close community the slanderer could be threatened with expulsion. In a big city he could be threatened with

34

as bad a fate. If every club member were reported to the secretary for uttering slanders about people of some importance which he could not prove to be true it would reduce the membership of a good many clubs.

All the blackmailer requires is information, and, if he pays for it, he will get it. And if he gets it, he can squeeze the slanderer unmercifully. As in the case of a City councillor, who was no better and no worse than the average man, but who, like the average man, had slandered his neighbour. And it was a deadly slander, a suggestion that a contractor had obtained work from the City corporation by corruption. It may have been true. These things do happen from time to time, but the councillor had no proof and should have kept his mouth shut unless and until he had such proof. And then should have mentioned it only to the proper authority, not, as he did, to a casual acquaintance after a good dinner at a big hotel. But a man in the position of a City councillor wouldn't do such a thing, you say. You may or may not be a councillor, but think what you have said under the influence of good food, wine and company. The conversation has been about corruption. You know something which your neighbour doesn't. The temptation to show off your knowledge is to many people very great and, though some of them resist it, some do not. If you like the majority of men in public life resist it. But that in all probability still leaves a substantial number of people who don't or can't resist it.

'Look, I shouldn't really be telling you this but – '. Have you never said that to anyone and never had it said to you?

One evening a man called on the councillor, Councillor Harvey Blair. Mr Blair was having dinner alone with his wife and did not relish an unexpected caller.

'My name is Penton,' said the caller. 'You won't know me but I've rather an urgent matter to discuss with you. May I come in?'

'What is it you want to see me about?'

'I'd rather discuss it privately in your study.'

'Why?'

'It's a private matter.'

'It's very inconvenient.'

'Oh, if it's inconvenient, I won't bother you,' said the stranger. 'As a matter of fact it's about Mr Lavender of the Lavender Construction Company.'

'Come in,' said Mr Blair. For the moment he thought that the stranger must have some interesting information about Mr Lavender.

He led Mr Penton to his study, after first telling his wife what had happened.

'What do you know about Lavender?' asked Blair, as soon as they were seated.

'What do you?' asked Penton.

'I haven't invited you in to answer questions,' said Blair. 'What have you come to tell me?'

'You don't care for Mr Lavender, do you, Mr Blair?'

'I repeat, you're not here to ask me questions.'

'Perhaps you're right,' said Penton. 'I'm here to make statements, not ask questions. Right. Statement No. 1. I represent an association of which you may not have heard, but it does very valuable work and is more necessary today than at any time in our history.'

'What association?'

'The Association for the Suppression of Slander.'

'There isn't such a thing.'

Mr Penton got up.

'I don't propose to be called a liar. Good evening.' He started towards the door.

'Just a moment,' said Blair. 'You mentioned Mr Lavender.'

'You called me a liar. Good evening.'

'Wait,' said Blair, 'what do you want with me?'

'To explain the objects and rules of our Association, but, as you don't believe in its existence, there seems little point in my staying.'

'I apologise,' said Blair. 'I was too hasty.'

'And not for the first time, if I may say so,' said Penton.

'What do you mean by that?'

'I'll tell you in due course. In the meantime would you like to know more about my Association?'

'Yes, I would.'

'Then you do believe in its existence?'

'You've told me it does exist.'

'But you said that was untrue.'

'I've apologised.'

'Certainly you've apologised. But that doesn't necessarily mean that you accept what I say. Do you believe I come from the Association?'

'If you tell me so, I accept it.'

'Then you accept that the Association exists.'

'That follows, I think.'

'Not perhaps as surely as the night the day,' said Penton, 'but sufficiently for present purposes.'

He sat down again and looked round the room.

'A nice place you have here.'

'Thank you.'

'Nothing garish about it. I can't understand why some hotels – good ones, I mean – have such terrible decorations. Take the Darlington, for instance. You know it, of course?'

'Yes.'

'Excellent food and service but what decorations! D'you know, the only tolerable place at the Darlington is the gents. The style there's not bad.'

'Perhaps you're right.'

'You know the gents there, of course.'

'Yes, I do.'

'Do you ever remember speaking about Mr Lavender in the gents?'

'How on earth can I remember a thing like that?'

'Let me help you. It was a public dinner at which you did not have to speak. Like many others you went out at half-time.'

'Well?'

'You mentioned Mr Lavender and a contract.'

'Did I?'

'Have you any evidence that Mr Lavender obtained a contract with the City corporation by corruption?'

'No, I haven't.'

'Then you don't suggest to me that he did?'

'No, I don't.'

'But under the influence of the good dinner at the Darlington you made that very suggestion.'

'How d'you know?'

'Because you were heard to do so.'

'I can deny it.'

'Of course you can. So can the man to whom you were speaking. But first of all isn't that rather an odd way for a City councillor to talk? I thought it was thugs and children who talked like that.'

'You can't prove I said it.'

'Oh dear, oh dear,' said Penton. 'You're worse than I expected. So, if we can't prove it, you'll deny it. So will the man you said it to – if you can remember who it was. Do you remember by the way?'

'It was – ', began Blair and then stopped short.

'You nearly fell for that one, didn't you? Anyway why beat about the bush? You know you said it, don't you?'

Blair did not answer.

'Well, I haven't all night,' said Penton. 'So I'd better help you to remember. If I tell you that my informant had a tape recorder with him would that jog your memory a bit?'

'It's scandalous.'

'Having a tape recorder, you mean?'

'Yes.'

'I rather agree. But which is the worse – taking away a man's character when he's not there to defend himself or getting a record of the man taking away the character? You don't say anything. Difficult question, I grant you.'

'What is your object in coming to see me?'

'I've told you partially. My Association is determined to do what it can to stop this kind of thing. It's bad enough when nonentities do it, but, when public men slander other people, it's far more serious. People take notice of what you say. Lavender might want to get on the Council himself one day. Fat lot of chance he'd have with you saying things like that about him. So we send agents round with small tape recorders and from time to time they hear people like you tell lies about other people.'

'Who says I was telling lies?'

'You do. You say you have no evidence that Lavender's corrupt. D'you want to repeat that he is, in spite of that.'

'I've said nothing about him to you.'

'Oh yes, you have. You've said that you don't suggest he's corrupt. What were you doing suggesting to an acquaintance that he was?'

'If I said it, I was talking loosely.'

'You can say that again. Loosely's the word. And what about the member of the Council Lavender's supposed to have corrupted? What would he think about it all?'

'I never mentioned his name.'

'No, that's true. You were prepared to slander Lavender. He wasn't a fellow councillor. But it just stuck in your throat to mention who the councillor was.'

'I repeat, what do you want of me?'

'If the Association decides to inform Mr Lavender, you'll not only have a big slander action brought against you, but you'll be shown to be a man who indulges in tittle-tattle of a highly dangerous sort. Not much more public life for you. And you like public life.'

'Well, what do you want me to do?'

'It's really the other way round. What do you want us to do? Give me a good reason why we shouldn't tell Mr Lavender. You see, we're not like you. You take away Lavender's character in his absence. At least we give you a chance of speaking up for yourself. Would you rather we told Lavender or not?'

'Of course I'd rather you didn't.'

'Give me a reason why we shouldn't.'

'Well, without boasting unduly, I think I lead quite a useful life. I pull my weight as a councillor.'

'Go on,' said Mr Penton. 'This is what I want to hear.'

'If a slander action is brought against me the publicity would probably ruin me. Would it be right to ruin a fairly useful public servant for opening his big mouth once too often?'

'D'you mean that this is the only occasion of its kind?'

'I've certainly never made a suggestion of this sort before.'

'You mean of corruption?'

'Yes.'

'You give me your solemn word that this is the only time you've accused a man behind his back of corruption when you'd no evidence of it.'

'I do.'

'Well, that's something,' said Penton and waited a short time before speaking again.

'These tape recorders are expensive,' he went on and brought out a small one from his pocket. 'Neat, aren't they? Don't try and take it from me. I'm bigger and stronger than you.'

'Anyway you have the other tape,' said Blair.

'As a matter of fact,' said Penton, 'I hate to confess it, but there isn't another tape. That, I'm afraid, was bluff. But this record is sufficient for my purposes.'

'Are these the normal methods used by your Association?'

'Lies, d'you mean? Certainly. We tell lies when necessary. Quite elaborate ones sometimes. We think the end justifies the means. People disagree about that and you're entitled to your own opinion. But we do send people round with tape recorders. As you can see. It just so happens that our informant didn't have one with him. However, that's academic now. Well, what else can you tell me? You say you've never charged anyone with corruption, but you're not saying you've never slandered anyone else over a drink or the dinner table or the like?'

'I suppose everyone does it from time to time.'

'Exactly. And that's the purpose of my Association. To stop this sort of thing. Can I report to my committee that you won't do it again?'

'Yes, you can.'

'What else can you suggest I should tell them to persuade them not to tell Mr Lavender? I should have mentioned that we're supported entirely by voluntary subscription.'

'Ah, I see,' said Blair. 'Now you're coming out into the open. I hope your tape is continuing to record. It'll be useful for the police.'

'Police?'

'You're about to invite me to subscribe to the association under the implied threat that, if I don't, you'll inform Mr Lavender of what I said about him. That's blackmail. And if you tell Mr Lavender, I'll tell the police.'

'Dear, dear,' said Penton. 'Which came first, the chicken or the egg? You seem to be threatening me with the police to prevent me from telling Mr Lavender.'

'That's right, I am.'

'Isn't that blackmail?'

'It isn't a crime,' said Blair, 'because I'm not trying to get any money out of you. You *are* trying to get money out of me.'

'I'm doing nothing of the kind. But in view of what you said there's no point in continuing our discussion. You ring the police straight away. Because I'm going to Mr Lavender straight away. Good evening.'

Penton got up to go. Blair thought hurriedly.

'I'm sorry,' he said. 'You win.'

'I don't do anything of the kind,' said Penton. 'I lose.' He walked towards the door. 'But so do you,' he added as he opened the door.

Blair telephoned the police and told them the whole story. A description of Penton was issued but without any results. He did not appear again to Blair, who was the only person who could identify him. He had given no address and, though an attempt was made to find out if there was an Association for the Suppression of Slander, it led to nothing, as was expected. On the other hand, a few days after the interview Blair received a letter from Lavender's solicitor threatening proceedings for slander. Lavender had been informed of the slander by an anonymous telephone call. After a certain amount of thought Blair reflected that it might have been cheaper to pay Mr Penton.

CHAPTER FIVE

The Trials of a Superintendent

Six months later Chief Superintendent Brookside, to whom the matter of the attempted blackmail of Councillor Blair had been referred, sent for an officer on his staff.

'Drew,' he said when the officer arrived. 'I think I've been particularly stupid. I expect it of you but not of myself.'

'Quite so, sir,' said Inspector Drew.

'Now, Drew,' went on the superintendent, 'make up a name of any kind for an association or institution for dealing with human weaknesses.'

'I beg your pardon, sir?'

The superintendent repeated his request.

'A name, sir?'

'Yes, a name.'

'What sort of name?'

'Any name you like. Here's an example – "The Society for Combating Human Weaknesses". That isn't what I want. It's too broad and general. But d'you see what I'm driving at?'

Inspector Drew had partly earned promotion by never pretending to understand something which he did not understand. Although he was sometimes cursed as a fool in consequence, the more intelligent of his superiors recognised this quality as a valuable one. It meant that the inspector, keen as he was, would be unlikely to apply, say, for a warrant for the arrest of a member of the Government, because he had not fully understood his instructions.

'No, sir,' he said.

'In that case of Councillor Blair the villain said he came from the "Association for the Suppression of Slander". There isn't such a thing, of course. You may remember we asked through the Press for people to come forward if they'd ever been approached by someone giving the name of this body.'

'Yes, I remember, sir.'

'And no one came forward.'

'Quite, sir.'

'Now make up several names like that, dealing with human weaknesses, either criminal or otherwise. Here's another example. It's not good but it should help to give you the idea. "The Society for Preventing Old Ladies being Robbed of their Money." That's much too unlikely. I want possible names, not absurd ones. The "Suppression of Slander" is a perfectly reasonable one. A good idea, in fact. Now go away and come back in half an hour with what I want.'

Half an hour later Inspector Drew was back with 'The Association for the Suppression of Crime' and 'The Association for the Suppression of Drunken Motorists'.

'Humph!' said the superintendent. 'Not brilliant, I'm afraid. You don't have to use the word "association" or "suppression". How about "The Society for the Prevention of Corruption of the Young"? That's a bit long.'

'May I ask what you want them for, sir?'

'You certainly may and you should have asked me before. I have a hunch that the gentleman who tried to squeeze Councillor Blair may have tried to squeeze other people. But he's going to use different names. It stands to reason. Blackmailers trade on human weaknesses, crime, adultery and so forth. And this ingenious fellow hit on slander. What I'm going to do and should have done before is to get the Press to invite people to come forward if anyone giving the name of an association like or similar to – then I shall set out the half-dozen suggestions I thought you'd bring to me. Blackmail's a terrible crime. You see, it's half ruined Councillor Blair. He refused to pay, so, to teach him a lesson, the blackmailer showed his teeth. He'll be able to quote that example to anyone else whom he may have approached under the name of the "Suppression of Slander Association". I may be wrong and nothing may come of it, but I ought to get the sack for not thinking of this idea before. That's what I'm paid for – partly anyway – to have ideas. So are you, Drew, and, if you want to become a superintendent, you'd better make some better suggestions than you have so far.'

In consequence of this interview a few days later the Press published a request to people to come forward if they had been approached by anyone giving the name of a society, club, institute or association like "The Society for the Prevention of Arson", "The Association for the Protection of Widows", "The Institute for the Discouragement of Vice".

'The name may be quite different from any one of these, which are simply quoted as examples. Anyone who has been asked to subscribe to any such society should come to Scotland Yard quoting this notice or go to his nearest police station. The maximum possible security and secrecy will be guaranteed.'

Hugh Bridges, who had been paying his £3 a week regularly and sorrowfully and with difficulty, read the superintendent's request in his newspaper. He did not want to make a fool of himself, so he wrote a letter to Scotland Yard asking 'if the Association for the Protection of the Public from Fraud' would do.

'Why didn't you think of that, Drew? I thought I was right. Go and see Mr Bridges at once and bring me back his story. And quick. We've lost a valuable six months. Though, as a matter of fact, that may not be a bad thing. This bird may think it's all blown over. Off with you and come back to me before you follow up anything he says.'

Two days later the superintendent was in possession of Hugh Bridges' story. In consequence, when a man called at the accommodation address which had been given to Hugh, to collect the envelope containing the three pounds, Inspector Drew and a sergeant were waiting for him.

'What's in that envelope?' said the inspector.

'Blessed if I know,' said the man. 'I was just told to collect it.'

'Who by?'

'By a man.'

'What man?'

'I know him as Ernie.'

'Where does he live?'

'No idea.'

'Then how will you give him this?'

'He'll meet me in the market.'

'What market?'

'Bermondsey.'

'When?'

'Tomorrow.'

'Very well,' said Inspector Drew. 'I'd like you to come to Scotland Yard with me at once.'

'What for?' asked the man. 'I've done nothing wrong.'

'If you haven't, you've nothing to worry about.'

'But why should I come?'

'Because I want you to.'

'Are you arresting me?'

'If you don't come willingly, I probably will. I have reason to believe that that envelope contains the sum of three pounds extracted from someone by threats.'

'Let's have a look and see if it does,' said the man.

'Are you coming with me or not? If you won't come voluntarily, I'll arrest you on suspicion of being the person concerned and put you up for identification. If you're only an innocent middle-man it'll help to clear you if you come along. Now which is it to be?'

'All right,' said the man. 'I'll come. But I swear I didn't know what was in it.'

Two hours later the superintendent interviewed the man, who said his name was Reynolds.

'All I know, sir, is that a couple of days ago a fellow asked me if I wanted to earn half a crown. I said: "How?" He said: "Fetching a letter. It's only ten minutes away." "Why can't you do it yourself?" I asked. "Do you want to earn half a crown or not?" he said. "I want to earn ten bob," I said. "Make it five," he said and I agreed.'

'And you've never done this before?'

'Well, to be truthful, guv, this is the second time.'

'You'd recognise this man again?'

'Sure.'

'Well, will you take us to him tomorrow?'

'There's no choice, is there?'

'No, there isn't. Now wait just a moment.'

The superintendent rang the bell and Hugh Bridges came in.

'Is this the man?' asked the superintendent.

'Oh no,' said Hugh. 'Nothing like.'

The superintendent sent Reynolds into another room and Hugh back to his home, while he discussed the matter with the inspector.

'What's to prevent Reynolds tipping off his chap if we let him go?'

'Nothing, sir. Very likely he will.'

'Then what are we to do? We've no real evidence to hold him. We'll have to persuade him. Bring him back again.'

And he was brought back.

'Now, Reynolds,' said the superintendent, 'if you lead us to this fellow you may need police protection. There are a lot of strong-arm men in the blackmail world.'

'I can look after myself, sir.'

The superintendent opened a drawer and pulled out a photograph of a dead man lying in a street, badly beaten up.

'Look at this,' he said. 'This fellow thought he could look after himself.'

Reynolds looked at the photograph.

'Nothing like that has ever happened to me,' he said.

'You wouldn't be sitting here at the moment,' said the superintendent, 'if it had. That man's dead. We're looking for his murderer. But, if we catch him, it'll be no consolation to the man on the pavement.'

'What d'you want me to do?'

'Stay the night here. It'll be quite comfortable. And then we'll go with you to Bermondsey tomorrow morning.'

'All right,' said Reynolds. 'If that's how you want it. It's better for me really because if I went off now and he didn't turn up, you'd say I'd given him the tip-off.'

"Well, there's that too,' said the superintendent. 'Look after him, inspector. I hope you'll be comfortable.'

The next morning Inspector Drew and a sergeant in plain clothes went to Bermondsey with Reynolds. But, before they reached the market they separated, Reynolds walking alone and the other two keeping him under observation from different places.

But no one approached Reynolds and he did not appear to give any warning sign to anyone. After waiting for an hour the inspector beckoned to Reynolds to come and talk to him.

'D'you think he'll come now?'

'I doubt it, guv'nor,' said Reynolds. 'He was dead on time last week.'

They waited for a further hour and then went back to Scotland Yard.

The superintendent wasn't pleased.

'He got wind of it somehow,' he said. 'Perhaps he saw you and the sergeant.'

'I don't think so, sir,' said the inspector, slightly nettled.

'Of course you don't *think* so, but a man doesn't forgo his weekly income without some good reason.'

'He may have been ill,' suggested the inspector.

'Then he'd have sent someone else. Well, we've achieved two things anyway. We've got Mr Bridges off the hook. They won't trouble him any more.'

'And the other, sir?'

'I'm glad you didn't give me time to tell you. You want to be impatient at this game. I know patience is important too, but unless you're impatient to get to the end of the road, the chances are you'll never get there. The second thing is that I believe these two cases are connected.'

'Why, sir?'

'First of all there's the same approach. The Institute or Association for this or that in each case. Secondly the mention of the word police and he makes himself scarce. As soon as Blair talked of the police, he was off and away. As soon as the police appear – because, whether you like it or not, Drew, you did *appear* – as soon as you appear, Bridges' man vanishes. And he won't come back.'

'Where does that leave us, sir?'

'*That* would leave us nowhere. But *this*,' and the superintendent brought out a piece of paper, 'will give us a lot of work to do. I'm going to use you entirely for this and let what's happened today be a warning to you. This is a very capable organisation. And I'm going to smash it. I hope with *your* help. If not, with someone else's.'

On the piece of paper were twelve names.

'These,' said the superintendent, 'are the fruits of my advertisement. And a very good crop too. We're on to a big thing here. And I want the villain or villains at the top. It'll take time and ingenuity and you may be bumped off in the process. Look at them. The Bankers' Protection Association, the Institute for Cleaner Morals and several more. Now go round and see these people as quickly as you can and bring me back a full report. This is a twenty-four-hour job. You can disturb me when you like. And don't, *don't*, whatever they may say to you – don't follow up anything on your own. It isn't that I don't trust your judgment, but, if there are going to be any mistakes made, *I*'m going to make them. In my opinion we're up against the biggest blackmail racket the country's ever known.'

So the inspector started on his job and was eventually joined by two more inspectors, for the work turned out to be far more than one or two men could do. There was a second and third crop of fruit from the superintendent's advertisement, with the result that eventually no less than a hundred and three cases of blackmail were discovered. It became quite clear that there was an organisation which was being most skilfully administered. The superintendent held his hand as long as he could before launching a single prosecution. As he had said, he wanted the man or men at the top, and, once prosecutions started, he feared he or they would disappear. Eventually he had to act. They had caught between twenty and thirty small fry, but, try as he would, he could not trace the people above them. They were all scared of the consequences of talking. So in due course they were prosecuted and received varying terms of imprisonment. But none of them would squeal.

As he had anticipated, the Press began to attack the police for not catching the real people behind the racket.

'It is obvious,' said one leading article, 'that there is a master brain behind all these cases. Until he is caught and put where he belongs no one will be safe. Blackmail is the foulest crime and only a few people who are blackmailed dare to go to the police. If the police have uncovered a hundred cases how many thousands must there be where the wretched victim dare not ask for help? If it is beyond the wit of the present chiefs of Scotland Yard to find out who is the man responsible, they should be replaced by people who can do it. Of course it may not be easy, but people are at the top because they are supposed to be capable of dealing with *difficult* problems.'

As Superintendent Pittville had been named as the officer in charge of the enquiries, he knew that the article was aimed at him. Instead of being annoyed he said to one of the assistant commissioners: 'The Press are quite right, you know. If I can't crack this one, I deserve to lose my job.'

The assistant commissioner said in one short word that the superintendent was talking nonsense and added: 'We can't always win. We can only do our best.'

'But our best ought to be good enough to deal with this case. Look at the villains we've brought in, and yet we can't get any further.'

'What the Press are urging us on to do,' said the assistant commissioner, 'is to bang these villains' heads against a wall until they will talk, and then they'd be the first to complain against our brutality. They only allow us to wear kid gloves and expect us to produce knuckle-duster results.'

'With the sort of kid gloves that my staff and I wear I still say we ought to be able to crack it. Twenty-eight of them and not a clue. I think we'll have to go out after the girl.'

'There's a girl in it, is there?'

'There is, and a very attractive one. Drew's a good-looking chap. Perhaps he'll be able to coax something out of her.'

'You've caught her, then?'

'Not yet. But I've hopes. She's in at least half a dozen cases. She ought to slip in one of them.'

'Good luck, then,' said the assistant commissioner.

The same day the superintendent sent for one of the men in custody who were charged with blackmail. His name was Walters and he was fairly well educated.

'I won't beat about the bush, Walters,' said the superintendent. 'I want your help.'

'And I won't beat about it either,' said Walters. 'You won't get it.'

'You don't know what it is yet.'

'That makes me even more certain.'

'You'll get seven years, you know, at least for this, maybe ten.'

'So?'

'So wouldn't it be nicer if it were five – even three – even nothing at all.'

'Much nicer.'

'Then it's up to you. If you help us, we can help you.'

'I heard from a man called Reynolds that you've a picture of a dead man in that drawer,' said Walters.

'Oh that,' said the superintendent. 'I've sent that away, but I've got another.'

'He talked too, I suppose.'

'There's only one thing I know for certain that he did. He died.'

'You can't stop people from dying, superintendent.'

'Nor can anyone.'

'Before their time, I mean. Unnatural Causes. A person or persons unknown.'

'You mean, if you talked, you'd want police protection.'

'Yes, for a time.'

'How long?'

'For the rest of my life.'

'You can have it.'

'Don't be absurd.'

'We'd send you abroad.'

'I don't want to go abroad. I want to live in peace in England where I was born. If I talk – and I don't say that I've got anything to talk about – but, if I talk, how long can you protect me fully in England?'

'We'd do all we could.'

'It wouldn't be enough. You know this game, superintendent, as well as I do – probably better. Frankly I'd prefer to go straight and live a peaceful, happy life. But it hasn't turned out that way. I don't like work, you see. I want all the ha'pence and none of the kicks.'

'You'll find ten years a pretty heavy kick.'

'Not worse than, say, being mangled by a motorcar. How could you stop that? I'm not going to live the rest of my life in one room or in a police car. Safety at that price wouldn't be worth it. And that's the only way I'd be sure of safety in this country.'

'Well, go abroad, then. There are lots of places to go to.'

'I only speak English.'

'You could go to America.'

'I don't particularly want to – but would they take me with my convictions?'

'We might be able to work it for you.'

'You might – and you might not. And anyway I don't want to go anywhere. The Isle of Wight's about as far away as I care to live.'

'That's about where you will be living for a good many years – but not very comfortably.'

'I shall manage.'

'And when you come out, what? There'll be no soft jobs waiting for you with all the ha'pence you want and all that ha'pence can buy. No one'll give you a decent job with your record. You'll be mixed up in some racket, and you'll be caught again and get another stretch.'

'But,' said Walters, 'for the weeks, months or years I'm out, I shall be free. I can do what I like, when I like, how I like. As I shall live by breaking the law, I don't have to worry about it. Of course I may be caught again, but, while I'm free, I'll be really free. Not like you are. You're not free, or anything like it. It's the lawbreakers who are free, while they're free. And it's worth a lot. How many of you know the real joy of freedom? There's nothing I'm frightened to do. I'll bet there are lots of things you'd like to do but can't, because you're a law-abiding citizen. Oh, it has its advantages, I'll grant you. But there are disadvantages too.

You're never free. While I'm out of prison, I'm free the whole time.'

'That's an interesting philosophy, Walters. It's a pity you won't put your obviously high intelligence to a better use.'

'Oh come, superintendent, you're not a judge yet. That's what they all say, those old fools. But they're even less free than you are. D'you remember Winston Churchill saying: "Who ever heard of a modern judge owning racehorses?" What's wrong with owning a racehorse? It's a free country. But it just isn't, except for chaps like me. So, sorry, superintendent, try someone else. You ought to find one.'

'Can you suggest who?'

'Yes,' said Walters. 'I could, but I'm afraid I won't even tell you that.'

'Look,' said the superintendent, 'I'll promise to do my level best to get you at least three years less, if you'll give me one name. And I'll keep my promise, whether I get anything out of him or not.'

'Superintendent,' said Walters. 'You're rattled. Buy yourself a drink.'

CHAPTER SIX

That Girl Again

For some months after the large number of prosecutions there was a lull – probably not in blackmail but in cases which came to the notice of the police. Then one day the superintendent had a call from a station sergeant at a police station.

'Excuse me, sir,' said the sergeant, 'but some months ago I was instructed to come direct to you if any case of blackmail was reported.'

'Quite right,' said the superintendent, 'what is it?'

'I've just had a call from a man who says he's being blackmailed by a girl at this moment. He could only speak for a second for fear she'd suspect something and leave. I've got the name and address.'

'Good man,' said the superintendent and, while he was taking particulars, rang all the bells in his office which would produce arms and legs and in some cases, in his opinion, not much more. Five minutes later he was on the way to The Elms in Mulberry Hill, SE23. He was told the front door would be left open. Five minutes before he arrived John Hardcastle was talking to the girl. It was the girl who had approached Mr Slaughter for the Institute for Cleaner Morals.

'Why d'you come here?' said Hardcastle. 'My wife might have been in.'

'I knew she wasn't. She's away for the weekend. Someone else is here though, someone of whom my Institute very much disapproves.'

'And you'll tell my wife about her unless I subscribe to the Institute?'

'*I* shall do nothing at all except report this interview to my principal.'

'But, unless you report that I'm a new subscriber, your principal will tell my wife I've been having an affair with another girl?'

'That's entirely a matter for my principal.'

'Suppose I told you my wife knows all about it and is herself having an affair of her own this very weekend?'

'Then I should tell my principal that you'd said that. I should also tell him that the second part of that statement isn't true. Your wife has gone to her sister.'

'The sister might be helping her.'

'What, with four children?'

'Well, the sister might be just a cover.'

'I expect you've got your sister-in-law's telephone number. If you haven't, I have. If you ring her, you'll find your wife's there.'

'You take a lot of trouble, don't you?'

'Cleaner morals are worth taking trouble about, whatever you may think about it.'

By this time the superintendent and a sergeant had entered the house and were listening outside the door. John Hardcastle thought he'd heard a slight movement.

'Just a moment,' he said. 'I thought I heard something.'

He said it loudly so that anyone listening could hear and be prepared for the door to open. He jumped up and flung the door open – the superintendent and sergeant had got out of sight. Hardcastle closed the door again.

'Funny,' he said. 'I could have sworn someone was listening at the door.'

'I suppose when you're having an affair,' said the girl, 'you get a bit edgy and think you can hear people in the passage.'

'How right you are,' said Hardcastle. 'It sounds as though you know from personal experience.'

'There's no need to be offensive,' said the girl.

'I'm not so sure about that,' said Hardcastle. 'You calmly walk into my house and say or imply that, if I don't subscribe five hundred a year to the Institute for Cleaner Morals, you'll tell my wife I'm having an affair with Eileen Abbot.'

'I never mentioned Eileen Abbot or five hundred pounds,' said the girl.

'That's quite true,' said Hardcastle. 'I was a bit in advance. But would £500 a year be thought a satisfactory subscription by your principal?'

'I should say it's quite generous,' said the girl.

'And, if I agree to subscribe, I can rely on the Institute not tipping off my wife?'

'I can only tell you that I'll report everything you've said to my principal.'

'And may I ask the name of your principal?'

'Certainly. His name is Jones.'

'Really? I hear the Joneses are just publishing their own telephone book. Any idea where I can find him?'

'He's not in the telephone book.'

'Is the Institute in it by any chance?'

'No, as I told you when I came here, our work is confidential.'

'That's why Mr Jones isn't in the book either, I suppose.'

'That's his business.'

'I suppose you couldn't give me any idea where I could contact Mr Jones. After all, without intending to be offensive – this time – you are only an agent, and, if I'm to subscribe £500, it's reasonable that I should meet your principal.'

'Certainly you shall. I'll take you to him myself.'

'Really?'

'Yes, really.'

The superintendent opened the door.

'Then perhaps we could all go together now,' he said.

He then explained who he was. He also noticed that the girl's attractiveness had not been exaggerated. She was very attractive indeed. He was quite glad that Inspector Drew had not been available and that he'd come himself.

'This is rather awkward,' said the girl. 'Mr Jones doesn't like police officers. I took one to him a few months ago and he was quite upset.'

'What is your full name, please?' said the superintendent.

'Why do you ask?'

'Because I'm proposing to arrest you and charge you with attempted extortion.'

'Oh, I shouldn't,' said the girl. 'Really I shouldn't.'

'You will now kindly come with me to Scotland Yard. And I must warn you that anything you say may be taken down and given in evidence.'

'All right,' said the girl, 'let's get going. I assume you have a car.'

The superintendent left the sergeant to take a full statement from Hardcastle and took the girl back to the car, which contained another sergeant and a driver.

The sergeant, left with Hardcastle, congratulated him.

'You were asking half the questions we'd like to ask. I assume, sir, that the information the girl had was quite wrong. That's why you weren't frightened to get in touch with us.'

'On the contrary,' said Hardcastle. 'The information the girl had was absolutely right. She was on a winner. I *am* having an affair with a girl and I'm terrified of my wife finding out. She chose the right victim exactly, except for one thing. She didn't know – she couldn't, as I didn't know it myself – that I'm a person who won't be blackmailed. I don't care what the consequences are. I simply won't stand for it. It was only when I realised what her game was that I also realised that I wasn't going to stand for it. So I made an excuse and said a few words to my local police station. I must say you fellows can act quickly. And you were smart too. I was terrified I'd throw open the door and there you'd be. Then you'd have heard nothing.'

'Well, I really do congratulate you, sir,' said the sergeant. 'If only everyone were like you, there'd be no blackmail. Now perhaps you'd make a full statement for me.'

Back at Scotland Yard the superintendent sent a car to fetch Inspector Drew and told him all about it before they interviewed the girl.

'We didn't talk at all in the car,' he said. 'She tried to make conversation, but I wouldn't be drawn. Much better to keep them waiting. Now let's have her in.'

'Before you charge me I'd like to have a word with the superintendent alone,' she said a few moments after she'd been brought in.

'Inspector Drew is handling this case with me,' said the superintendent.

'No doubt,' said the girl, 'but, if you want information out of me, I'd like to speak to the superintendent alone.'

'Very well then, will you leave us, please, inspector.'

The inspector left and the superintendent and the girl were together for an hour and a half. When the inspector was summoned to the superintendent's room again, she was gone.

'I gather it went well, sir,' the inspector said. 'She's down below now, I suppose.'

'She's gone home,' said the superintendent.

'Gone home!!' said the inspector.

'Yes. I think I may have been a bit hasty.'

'Hasty, sir? But you had ample evidence on which to charge her. It was open and shut.'

'Perhaps you'll leave it to me to judge what is open and what is shut,' said the superintendent.

The inspector thought for a moment.

'Oh, I see, sir,' he said, 'you hope she'll lead you on to someone important? Have you put a tail on her?'

'Really, Drew, I don't expect you to cross-examine me about what I do. No, I have simply let her go. As I said, I think I acted too hastily.'

'Well, I don't understand it, sir,' said the inspector.

'There are a lot of things you don't understand, Drew.'

'Yes, sir,' said Drew, 'and this is one of them.'

'Don't be impertinent.'

'I'm sorry, sir, but it's so puzzling.'

'Well, stop being puzzled and go home.'

'Very good, sir.'

Inspector Drew left the superintendent's office in a very troubled frame of mind. He was deeply worried. He could not believe that a man of the superintendent's years of experience and integrity could fall for a girl, however attractive, but he could think of no other solution. A sprat to catch a mackerel would have been quite intelligible. But then a watch would have to be kept on the girl. They knew nothing about her. Whatever she had told the superintendent might be completely untrue. You can't trust girls like her. And the superintendent just let her go when she'd been caught red-handed. It simply didn't make sense, whatever way you looked at it. The superintendent was a hard-headed, unemotional sort of chap. He couldn't possibly fall for a pretty face and good figure, even if they'd been superlative. And if he'd been a stupid man, unfit for his job, he wouldn't have done such a thing in the presence of so many witnesses. There were at least four people who knew he'd arrested the girl. She was probably a high-class tart. And he'd just let her go. It was extremely odd. And then he remembered with a shock that there had been a Minister of the Crown who'd made a fool of himself over a girl. But not a girl he'd just seen once. Of course there has to be a first meeting, he told himself. But it was impossible. He didn't know anyone in the Force whom he'd suspect of corrupt motives, and it was unbelievable in the case of the superintendent. And yet. And yet. Why had he let her go?

CHAPTER SEVEN

The Trial Begins

Three months later the same girl was walking across a road arm-in-arm with a man, when a dark saloon car drove straight at them. The man pushed the girl out of the way so that she fell on to the pavement and was slightly bruised, but he himself was knocked down and badly injured. The girl became almost distraught, thinking he was dead. An ambulance was called and they were both taken to hospital. No one had been able to take the number of the car, which went off at speed.

And a fortnight later the trial began. Not of the driver of the car, whose identity was never discovered for certain, but of a man called Clifton Ledbury, for conspiracy to blackmail. He was the man who, if the police were right, was the person for whom the superintendent had been looking. And at last, if the evidence was to be relied upon, he had been found. On the face of it he was anything but a blackmailer. He had a legitimate export and import business in the City, he owned a house in London and was a member of several respectable clubs. He was quite a good golfer and had plenty of reputable friends. If he was guilty, he must have conducted his criminal affairs wholly unknown to his friends. There are such people and every now and then you get a shock when you find that that very pleasant fellow with whom you've often had a drink, obtained a substantial part of his income by letting flats to prostitutes. So the drinks you accepted from him were indirectly paid for by immoral earnings.

The trial took place at the Old Bailey. The judge was Mr Justice Hereford, a man of sixty-five, a widower with a young daughter often called Angela. He had married late in life and his wife had died when Angela was born. The judge was devoted to her and, as she grew older, she began to console him for the loss of his wife. She was an attractive, intelligent girl and even at the age often could carry on a conversation on a level of intelligence beyond that of a normal child of her age. And his whole world outside the courts centred on her, and she adored him. He was her father and her mother.

Before the trial started he was in his room talking to his clerk.

'What'll you give this chap?' asked his clerk. 'Twenty years?'

'John,' said the judge, 'you never seem to learn. If I allowed my mind to think about sentencing a man before he was convicted, I might very well – even unconsciously – try to steer the course of the trial towards a conviction.'

'Well, you wouldn't be the first,' said John.

'I dare say not,' said the judge. 'But I think we've improved a bit since the old days. There are far fewer hanging judges today than there used to be.'

'You don't get the chance,' said John.

'You know quite well what I mean. Most judges are fair today. Don't you think so?'

'Oh – very fair,' said John. 'They just sum up – most fairly, of course – for a conviction.'

'Am I like that?' asked the judge.

'You're pretty good on the whole, I will say, sir,' said John. 'But I hope you're not going to be fair in this case. If this chap gets away with it, it'll be a scandal. He's wrecked more lives than Hitler.'

'That's nonsense,' said the judge. 'But, if he's guilty, it is a very bad case, I grant you.'

'Well, you put him away, so that he can't do it again. He's defending himself, I'm told. Why d'you think that is?'

'I've no idea,' said the judge. 'It can't be the expense. Apparently he's well-to-do.'

'D'you think he hopes to get the sympathy of the jury? He's quite a good-looking bloke.'

'That is possible. If he's conducting his own case, they'll hear far more from him than if he were represented. Usually a jury only hear a man give his own evidence. But, if a man makes a good impression, he can make much more of himself if he cross-examines all the witnesses and makes a speech to the jury as well as giving evidence. Of course, it cuts both ways. If he makes a bad impression on them, he'll be digging his own grave.'

'Well, let's hope he makes a bad impression. He's guilty all right, isn't he? You've read the depositions.'

'Yes, of course, but there's always some sort of a case against a man on the depositions or the case couldn't get as far as trial. When one analyses the evidence I've read, it really all depends on one witness.'

'Margaret Vane, you mean?'

'Yes. If she isn't believed, I don't see how the jury can convict.'

'But, from what I heard about the case in the Temple, there is some other evidence, isn't there?'

'A little, but without the girl it comes to nothing. And it's quite a tall order to get a conviction for a vast conspiracy on the evidence of one witness.'

'You think he's guilty, don't you?' asked John.

'Quite frankly,' said the judge, 'until I've heard him and the girl I can't possibly form an idea. Obviously the police *think* he's the man, and they're more often right than wrong, but like all of us, they make mistakes. As you say, if he is convicted, he's bound to get a very long sentence. Are they ready for us yet? I don't like starting big cases as late in the afternoon as this.'

It was just after three o'clock. The judge had tried another case earlier in the day. It had finished at just after 2.30 pm. Normally Ledbury's case would have come on straightaway but he had asked for a short adjournment and the judge had granted it.

At 3.15 pm, however, the prisoner was ready. Mr Justice Hereford came in and the trial began. Ledbury had already pleaded not guilty, so the jury were sworn, the clerk read out the indictment and counsel for the Crown, Henry Stokes QC, rose to open the case. The case was such a bad one that the Director of Public Prosecutions had considered with the Attorney-General whether he or the Solicitor-General ought to prosecute, but it would have been very inconvenient for either of them at the time and so Henry Stokes was briefed. He was an able member of the Criminal Bar with most of the virtues and some of the vices of advocates who practise almost entirely in the English criminal courts.

'Members of the jury,' he began, 'as you have heard, the prisoner is charged with one offence only, conspiracy to extort money from people. But, though only one offence is charged, the evidence will disclose to you a plot to blackmail people up and down the country on a vaster scale than has ever been heard of before. The word "blackmail" does not occur in any Act of Parliament but it is the word commonly used to describe the crime with which the accused is charged. Strictly speaking he is not charged with any particular act of blackmail but, in fact, with something far worse, namely with being the head of a blackmail organisation. There are various forms of extortion which are prohibited by law. In this case the extortion was by threatening to publish or refrain from publishing something about the victim in order to extort money from him. Before I come to the details of the case I will tell you how the accused's organisation worked, and it may well make you shudder. Up and down the country in every walk of life the accused had agents collecting information about other people. No one who had ever done anything of which he might be ashamed, or which he might not want to get to the ears of someone else was safe. Of course, the accused preferred the more luscious fruit – such as a pools winner who, having won £100,000, spent some of it in riotous living, the nature of which he did not want disclosed to his wife. He was an obvious target. One of the accused's agents paid someone in a night club to give the information and within a few days the blackmailer was on his way to squeeze this unfortunate pools winner, who soon wished he'd never seen a football pool coupon. I have so far referred to these actions as being done by the accused, but I should make it plain that he did not do any of the dirty work himself. He was, until found out, a respectable business man. But he had two lieutenants, a man called Jones and another man called Nottingham. Jones was in charge of the collection of information side. Nottingham was in charge of the collection of money side. Each of those two lieutenants had an army of agents and sub-agents under him, particularly Jones. The collection of information does not require so much skill as the collection of money. There are few people who have never done anything that they would not wish to be known – at any rate by one other person. Jones employed his army of agents to collect such information. To take a simple example, a clerk in a bookmaker's office gave information to one of Jones' agents that a bank clerk was backing horses regularly. As you probably know, bank clerks are forbidden to gamble. So this young man, who had a very promising career ahead of him, was squeezed unmercifully, until eventually he went to the police. Now what I may call the Jones and Nottingham sides of the business were quite distinct. What Jones and his agents had to do was to provide information. Nottingham and his agents did the rest. Though, once again, the head man – Nottingham – never, so far as is known, did the actual blackmailing. He simply controlled the operation. Now this side of the business required far more skill. It's easy enough to pay a club doorman or a strip-tease girl for information about Mr X. But to persuade Mr X to pay to prevent that information being passed on to someone else requires a number of qualities, in particular nerve and quick thinking. It was, therefore, not so easy for Nottingham to get sufficient agents to carry out his side of the business. And there were casualties, for from time to time the victim squealed and the blackmailer was caught. Someone else had to be found to do the work. It was highly paid, but the amount of money ultimately finding its way into the hands of the accused must have been enormous. I shan't be able to prove how much. But the organisation spread its net so wide that its annual income – all free of tax – must have been very large indeed. Every walk of life was invaded, the factories, the trade unions, local government, Members of Parliament, the professions, doctors, clergymen, village institutes, boards of directors, even the schools and universities. One wretched undergraduate was eventually driven by the blackmailer's demands to suicide.

'I have referred to Jones' agents. These people were often comparatively innocent in the first instance. And, indeed, some remained so. Over a pint of beer they may have given away all that was required and may never have come into the transaction again. No one was too small to be a potential victim. If a man could pay – say £2 a week out of his wages – he would do very nicely. £200 was, of course, much better but £2 would do. When I tell you that over two hundred cases came to the notice of the police, and there were successful prosecutions in nearly a hundred of these cases, how many cases do you think there may have been which never did come to the notice of the police? That is the blackmailer's weapon. Fear. How can you be sure that your wife will never know if you go to the police? Many victims daren't. I doubt if an iceberg has anything like as much below the surface as this terrible tale of proved extortion. Now it is no part of my duty to try to influence you against the accused by dwelling on the horrible nature of his crime. Blackmail has been called moral murder. It drains the soul out of a man.'

At this point the prisoner stood up.

'My lord,' he said, 'if it's no part of counsel's duty to talk about moral murder and so forth, why does he do it? I quite agree with all he says about blackmail, but the question the jury has to try is whether these abominable crimes are anything to do with me. I strongly repudiate the suggestion.'

Before the judge could say anything, Stokes went on: 'Mr Ledbury is quite right, my lord. I was a little carried away by the depth of infamy the facts in this case disclose.'

'When you talk about depth of infamy, aren't you doing it again, Mr Stokes?' said the judge.

'I apologise, my lord,' said Stokes, 'and it is really very stupid of me. The facts themselves in this case will speak with far more deadly force than anything out of my poor vocabulary.'

'Thank you, Mr Stokes,' said Ledbury. 'And while you're about it – '

'Please don't interrupt, Mr Ledbury,' said the judge. 'You've made your point and counsel has conceded it.'

'My lord,' said Ledbury, 'I only wanted to ask how counsel was proposing to prove all these things against me. My name isn't Jones or Nottingham. He says I'm responsible for something. He oughtn't to say that, unless he thinks he can prove it.'

'I am going to prove it,' said Stokes, 'but I can't tell the jury everything in one sentence. Members of the jury, I was telling you the set-up of this vast organisation. How many people were employed I cannot tell you, but at the head, the prosecution say, was the accused, well away from the scene of battle and a man commanding so much evil and having such power to strike – always through others – that, when his subordinates were caught, they dared not give away information as to the other people concerned with them. I mentioned a number of prosecutions. In none of those cases was the person accused prepared to help the police in any way. They did not want to be imprisoned, as many of them were, for considerable periods, but they feared something else even more, vengeance on the squealer. Below the accused came Jones and Nottingham, who until a very late stage formed an impenetrable barrier between him and the police. I shall return to Jones and Nottingham a little later, but, first of all, I want to take up the challenge of the accused. "How are you going to prove all this?" he asks. "You say I kept away from the scene of battle. How then can you prove it was me rather than one of a million other people?" Well, members of the jury, if you were concerned to find out who was behind a vast conspiracy like this, how would you set about it? You remember the Great Train Robbery. Whose was the brain behind that? No one knows for certain. There is only one way in which it could have been found out. By infiltrating someone into the conspirators' army. By employing a man or woman to enter the ranks of the criminal army and to work his way to the top. A very dangerous and difficult job. A very unpleasant one too, for it would involve the person concerned in doing many most distasteful acts. He would have to act like a soldier in that army, do the things that other soldiers did, lie like a trooper when necessary and all the time with the knowledge that, if discovered, his life would be forfeit. Just like a spy in wartime. And believe me, members of the jury, although this country is at peace externally, there are violent internal wars being waged the whole time between the police and the criminal community. And this particular war was considered one of the most important, there being comparatively few people in the country who in the end would be safe from the blackmailing activities of this gang. Is there not at least one of you, members of the jury, who might be prepared to pay to prevent information on a particular matter reaching someone you know? If everyone had a perfectly clear conscience, members of the jury, the blackmailer would have no chance.'

'Mr Stokes,' intervened the judge, 'don't overdo it. I'm only an ordinary man with the usual human frailties, but I can think of nothing in respect of which I could be blackmailed. Nor, I suspect, could you. Or the clerk of the court. I really don't know why you should accuse the jury of being criminals or adulterers or at any rate people who have done something so wrong that they are terrified of it being disclosed. Of course we all do wrong from time to time. We are all sinners. But I doubt if the average Englishman commits adultery, or does any of the other things which provide the blackmailer with useful material. There are about fifty million people in the country. If a hundred thousand of those provide scope for extortion that is a sufficiently large number but it is only one in five hundred of the population. Not one in twelve or anything like it.'

'I'm sorry, my lord,' said Stokes. 'Perhaps I did exaggerate.'

'There's no "perhaps" about it,' said the judge. 'I think you should apologise to the jury for suggesting that one of them is a scallywag. How many judges are there? Between a hundred and two hundred including county court judges. Many more than twelve. How many of them are you suggesting are fit subjects for blackmail?'

'I'm sorry, my lord.'

'The reason I intervened,' went on the judge, 'was not just because you were grossly exaggerating, but because in a sense you were threatening the jury. "Let this man go free", you were almost saying, "and see what happens at any rate to one of you." That is a most undesirable way in which to present the case to the jury. Your duty is to open the facts, fairly and without exaggeration and without indulging in any high-flown prejudicial flights of fancy, let alone threatening the jury with the consequences to themselves of an acquittal.'

'I do apologise to your lordship and the jury,' said Stokes.

'Thank you, Mr Stokes, I felt sure I had only to mention the matter for you to appreciate what you had been doing. Now pray continue.'

'Well, members of the jury,' said Stokes, 'that is how the accused was unmasked. A courageous young woman, Miss Margaret Vane, was found who was prepared to run the risk of discovery in order to find out who was behind it all. She was not employed in the first instance by the police; indeed, even when at a later stage the police discovered her activities, at her special request they did not intervene. She feared that, once the police were known to be concerned, the head or heads of the organisation would disappear. This young woman was in fact employed by a journalist who, with the help of a large daily newspaper, was seeking to do what the police had been unable to do. She is the witness on whom the prosecution mainly relies. She can give direct evidence of the accused's guilt. If you believe her, you will have no doubt whatever of the accused's guilt. And she has lived to tell the truth, though you may think she has been lucky.'

'What does counsel mean by that?' asked Ledbury.

'Yes,' said the judge, 'what do you mean?'

'She was nearly killed by a car, my lord.'

'That has happened to many of us,' said the judge.

'This was deliberate, my lord.'

'But have you any evidence that the attempt was anything to do with the accused?'

Stokes hesitated.

'I must confess, my lord, that I haven't,' he said after a moment.

'Then you should never have mentioned it to the jury. Members of the jury, please dismiss from your minds any suggestion that the accused had anything to do with this motorised attack on the lady.'

'Now, members of the jury,' went on Stokes, 'I come back to Jones and Nottingham. You may ask why they are not in the dock with the accused. Members of the jury, I wish they were. But after they had been traced and questioned and made statements, they disappeared. Whether they have fled the country, whether they are alive or dead, we do not know. In fairness to the accused, members of the jury, I cannot read out the statements which they made but – '

'Really, my lord,' protested Ledbury, 'this is too much. The words "in fairness to the accused" ought to have stuck in Mr Stokes' throat. What he is trying to suggest to the jury is that statements, which he knows quite well are not evidence against me, in fact implicate me in some way.'

'I didn't say they implicated you,' said Stokes.

'Then why mention them at all?' said the judge. 'A lot of people have made statements. Why mention that Jones and Nottingham made statements?'

'They *made* statements, my lord.'

'I repeat,' said the judge, 'so did a lot of other people. Statements are being made all day long but you don't refer to them. Why refer to those of Jones and Nottingham, if they're irrelevant?'

'Oh, they're not irrelevant, my lord. They are simply not admissible under our rules of evidence.'

'This is worse than ever, my lord,' said Ledbury. 'Mr Stokes now says the statements are relevant to the case, but *in fairness* to me he mustn't read them out. It's really too bad. And then, did you notice, my lord, the way in which he gave a half-glance at me when he said that he did not know if Jones or Nottingham are dead. And this came shortly after he'd said how lucky the woman in the case is to be alive. He is plainly trying to suggest to the jury that I try to make away with witnesses, either personally or through someone else. Before he's finished he'll be warning the jury that I'll make away with them if they don't acquit me. Or even you, my lord.'

'Don't you overdo it either, Mr Ledbury,' said the judge. 'There is much merit in your protest but you don't improve it by silly exaggerations. But I'm not happy about this, Mr Stokes. Mr Ledbury, would you prefer to have a fresh trial before a new jury, when I trust the case will be properly and fairly opened?'

Ledbury thought for a moment.

'My lord, if you will let me say a word to the jury now, I shall be content for the trial to continue.'

'Well, it's very unusual,' said the judge, 'but, in view of what's happened, you may. But keep it short, please.'

'Thank you, my lord,' said Ledbury. He turned towards the jury.

'Members of the jury,' he said, 'counsel for the prosecution is well aware that the case against me is of the flimsiest nature, and he is trying to make up for his lack of evidence by tricks of the kind which you have heard. Everyone hates a blackmailer. Hate me by all means, if I am one. But I say that I am not.'

'Very well,' said the judge, 'now let's get on.'

'Members of the jury,' continued Stokes, 'I should like to apologise yet again to you and to the accused. In this country it is no part of the duty of the prosecution to seek to secure a conviction at all costs. My only duty is to seek to put before you as fairly as I can the facts which the prosecution claim to be able to prove. If, when you have heard the whole of the evidence in the case – not simply the evidence for the prosecution but that for the defence as well – if, when you have heard all this evidence you have any reasonable doubt about the matter it will be your pleasure to acquit the accused. I say "pleasure" because although, as Mr Ledbury has said, everyone hates a blackmailer, even more important than sending a blackmailer to prison for many years is making sure that an innocent man is not sent to prison at all. In this country we have been able to devise no better safeguard against such a calamity – for that is what a wrong conviction is – a calamity of the first order, which is horrifying to us all – we have been able to devise no better safeguard than never to convict an accused person unless we are sure of his guilt, unless we can put our hands on our hearts and say "there is no reasonable doubt but that this man is guilty". Sometimes people talk about giving the benefit of the doubt to a person accused of crime. His lordship may tell you that that is quite a wrong way of putting the matter. The accused is entitled as a matter of right – not as a matter of clemency, or bounty or some other benefit but as a matter of right – he is entitled to be acquitted if the prosecution fails to prove its case with that measure of certainty to which I have already referred.'

'Mr Stokes,' intervened the judge, who had been getting fidgety at Stokes' prolixity, 'no doubt one day you will be a judge and will have the opportunity of instructing juries on the law of proof in criminal cases, but I fancied that that was my province at the moment. Your duty is to outline to the jury the evidence which you are about to call, isn't it?'

Stokes smiled ruefully. He was not, in fact in the least put out. Indeed he rather enjoyed mild skirmishes with the Bench. He had also enjoyed Ledbury's interventions. They had assisted rather than hindered him. He had successfully introduced all the prejudice against the prisoners and Ledbury's complaints had enabled him to show what a fair man he was.

'My lord,' he said, 'it seems that I can't do right in this case. Either I offend Mr Ledbury or your lordship.'

'You don't offend me in the least, Mr Stokes,' said the judge. 'I merely thought that we might as well get on with the case. The jury don't want it prolonged more than is necessary. It makes no difference to me. If I'm not trying this case, it will be some other.'

'In other words, my lord,' said Stokes, 'your lordship considers that I have been wasting time.'

'Your interpretation is correct, Mr Stokes.'

'Well, it's nice to be right occasionally,' said Stokes. 'I hope your lordship will forgive me.'

'Only if you get on now,' said the judge.

'Very well, my lord. Members of the jury, I am not calling many witnesses but you may think that it is the quality of the witnesses which counts, not their quantity. The most important is, of course, Miss Vane. I freely grant the accused that, if you do not find her an acceptable witness, the case for the Crown collapses. I shall also call before you the superintendent of police, who interviewed the accused before his arrest. You may think his evidence will to a small extent corroborate Miss Vane's. But first of all I shall call before you two of the victims. I am calling them for two reasons. First to give examples of how this horrible trade was plied and secondly because, although, as I have already indicated, the accused had no direct contact with any of these victims, I hope to prove that he had inside knowledge about them, which he could only have had if he had been involved in the conspiracy. I will call Hugh Bridges.'

CHAPTER EIGHT

The First Two Witnesses

Hugh came into the court looking as miserable as he felt. His entrance into court and to the witness box was even more pitiful than it might have been, as he had recently sprained his ankle. His clothes were shabby and his pronounced and obviously painful limp added to his general appearance of unhappiness. He apologised to the judge for his slowness and explained the reason. Then he took the oath and waited apprehensively for his examination to begin. It was not that he feared any particular question but the proceedings in court frightened him, as they do other people.

The legal profession does not always realise what an ordeal it may be for some people, who have never been in a court before, to be called into the witness box. Judges, barristers and many solicitors are so used to the inside of a court that its effect upon those who have come there for the first time is not always appreciated. If it were, witnesses would be offered seats in the witness box and the form of oath would be made easier to say and to comply with. As it is, it sometimes happens that a nervous witness has already stumbled several times over the oath before he or she is ready to answer counsel's first question. Whatever results may be obtained outside court by strong-arm methods in the quest for truth, it is less likely to be obtained from a witness who has been reduced to a jelly before the questioning has even started. Moreover it seems rather hard on a witness who firmly believes in Almighty God that he should be compelled to swear by Him that he will tell the whole truth, when the law of evidence does not permit him to do so.

Stokes took Hugh through his unhappy story from beginning to end. Then Ledbury was asked by the judge if he would like to cross-examine.

'Yes, please, my lord,' he said, and looking towards Hugh, began his questions.

'Now, Mr Bridges,' he said, 'everyone's supposed to be very sorry for you – the jury particularly. Let's see if they ought to be. Did you have a decent home as a boy?'

'Very,' said Hugh.

'Your parents were happy together? No broken marriage – nothing of that sort?'

'No.'

'And you had a good education, went to church and all that?'

'Yes.'

'Never went short of food or clothes when you were a boy?'

'No.'

'Or love?'

'Love?'

'Your parents were fond of you and you of them?'

'Certainly.'

'And, when you grew up, you started to instruct the young?'

'Yes.'

'And not finding the salary enough you tried to earn some extra money in the holidays?'

'I've said so.'

'And then you took to getting the money by fraud?'

'What do you expect me to say to that?'

'I expect you to agree.'

'It's quite unnecessary to bully the witness, Mr Ledbury,' said the judge.

'He's not in the dock, my lord,' said Ledbury. 'I am. I'm simply trying to expose a bit of revolting sob-stuff for what it is. If this fraudulent trickster hadn't had a chance in the world there'd be some reason to be sorry for him. But he's no excuse at all. And he's simply put into the witness box to make the jury angry and to vent their anger on me.'

'Don't make speeches,' said the judge. 'Have you any further questions to ask?'

'Yes, my lord, I have. Have you seen me before, Mr Bridges?'

'No, I haven't.'

'Have you any reason in the world to think that I had anything to do with your experiences – except that you see me here in the dock?'

'I can't say that I have.'

'Then why on earth are you called as a witness, I'd like to know?'

'I didn't want to come. This is one of the days I address envelopes,' said Hugh sadly.

That was the only employment which he had been able to obtain. He had resigned from his school when he went to the police.

'There's no need to whine about it. What's wrong with addressing envelopes?'

'If you have any proper questions to ask,' said the judge, 'ask them, but I am not going to allow this bullying to go on any longer.'

'My object is to show to the jury that this witness ought never to have been called.'

'If at the end of the case his evidence is irrelevant to your guilt or innocence I shall tell the jury so,' said the judge.

'Thank you, my lord,' said Ledbury and he sat down.

'That is all, Mr Bridges,' said Stokes.

'Thank you.'

Hugh left the witness box and took a seat in court.

'Call David Bentley,' said Stokes.

A young man went into the witness box and took the oath.

'How old are you?' he was asked by Stokes.

'Twenty-one.'

'Are you interested in sport?'

'Very.'

'What are your greatest interests?'

'Tennis and rowing.'

'I believe you're quite good at both.'

'They say so,' said the boy.

'You mustn't be too modest about it,' said Stokes. 'Did you qualify for Wimbledon?'

'Well, yes, I did.'

'But you never played there?'

'No.'

'I'll ask you the reason for that a little later on. Now what about rowing?'

'I was very keen on it.'

'Yes, we know. Any particular aspect of rowing that interested you most?'

'Yes, sculling. I wanted to go in for the Diamonds.'

'That's a sculling race at Henley, I believe?'

'Yes, it is.'

'Were you qualified to enter for it?'

'I think I would have been.'

'You never did enter for that race?'

'No.'

'I want to ask you something about your father. Is he a wealthy man?'

'I suppose he is.'

'Did he give you an allowance?'

'A very small one.'

'Were you at a university?'

'Yes – I was.'

'Did you find difficulty in paying your way on your father's allowance?'

'I was a bit extravagant, I suppose. Yes, I did find it difficult to manage.'

'Did you find some way of supplementing your income?'

'Yes.'

'What was it?'

'I started to coach some of the boys and girls near where I lived in the vacations.'

'They paid you?'

'Yes, on the quiet, of course.'

'Why on the quiet?'

'Because it affected my amateur status.'

'Please explain in a little more detail. Some of the jury may not know about it.'

'Well, at that time you were not supposed to accept money.'

'Accept money for what?'

'For playing games or coaching.'

'What happened if you did?'

'You couldn't compete in amateur tournaments.'

'Do you mean that, if it had been discovered by the All-England Lawn Tennis Club that you'd coached for money, you couldn't have played at Wimbledon?'

'That's right. I couldn't have rowed at Henley either.'

'What's rowing got to do with tennis?'

'Nothing. But, if you want to compete as an amateur in rowing, you must not be a professional in any sport. A tennis coach couldn't compete at Henley.'

The judge intervened.

'Could a professional cricketer compete at Wimbledon before it became open?' he asked.

'I don't know, my lord,' said the boy.

'Well, I'm glad it doesn't matter now,' said the judge. 'Now that they have an open tournament at Wimbledon, I mean.'

'Anyway,' went on Stokes, 'by taking money for coaching you disqualified yourself from competing at Wimbledon and Henley?'

'Yes, I did. But I hoped to keep it quiet. And then everything would have been all right.'

'Why didn't you in fact compete at Wimbledon?'

'Eventually I had to tell them about my coaching.'

'How did that come about?'

'Well, it's a long story,' said the boy.

'I know it is,' said Stokes, 'but that's why we're here. Tell my lord and the jury your long story.'

'Well,' said the boy, 'it started one day when I saw a man watching me give another boy lessons on a public court. I didn't take any notice of him at first, but, while I was on the way home, he came up to me.'

'What did he say?'

'He said he'd seen me at the courts and he thought I must be jolly good. "At any rate you're a jolly good coach," he said. "Would you give me any lessons?" "I only coach friends," I said. "Why's that?" he said. "You could make a lot more teaching strangers. I'd pay well." "I don't take money for it," I said. "Don't you?" he said. "What did I see that young man hand you when you said goodbye?" I got angry. "What the hell has that got to do with you?" I said. "A good deal, I'm afraid," he said. "Have you ever heard of the Anti-Shamateur League?" "No, I haven't," I said. "Well you have now," he said. "I'm one of the Committee. You don't read anything about us, as we try to keep our work as confidential as possible. It's best for everyone. Now don't let's beat about the bush. I know all about you." '

The boy paused.

'Go on,' said Stokes.

'I was trying to think,' said the boy. 'It's not all that easy to remember.'

'Of course it isn't,' said the judge. 'Take your time.'

'Oh yes, I remember,' said the boy. 'He went on to say that he knew I had ambitions to play at Wimbledon and scull at Henley and that I had a good chance of doing both. "Well," I said, "what about it?" "There's this about it," he said. "I happen to know that you've disqualified yourself from competing at either. You're a professional coach." "I'm nothing of the sort," I said. "I just take a bit of money from friends for helping them." "I'll write that down," he said and he wrote it down. When he'd done so, he said that what I was doing was just the same as being a professional coach. Being a professional simply meant that you took money for it. It didn't matter, he said, whether you took it from friends or enemies, so long as you took it. Of course I knew he was right and that I shouldn't have done it, but doing it in such a small way I thought it didn't really matter.'

'And you wanted the money?' Ledbury suddenly asked.

'Be quiet,' said the judge. 'You'll be able to cross-examine in due course. Meantime behave yourself.'

'Well, what happened?' asked Stokes.

'He went on to say,' said the boy, 'that his league sympathised very much with people in my position. He said he'd try to help me if he could. I asked what he meant. I didn't need his help, I said. "Don't you?" he said. "If I report this matter to my committee without any recommendation in your favour, you'll simply be reported to the authorities and bang will go your chances of competing at Wimbledon or Henley." I asked why they should report me and he repeated that he came from the Anti-Shamateur League. "What d'you think the name stands for?" he asked. "What's the good of having a league like this unless it does something to justify the name? We find out cases like yours and report them." "I thought you said you wanted to help me," I said. "That would ruin my chances." "I'm glad you realise that," he said. "Yes, we do try to help young people like you, if we can. But we've got to be sure we're doing the right thing." I asked him what he wanted. "Well, it's for my committee to say," he said. "I'm only one member. But we've got to satisfy ourselves, first, that you're worth helping and secondly that, if we let you off this time, it will never, never happen again." "I promise," I said. "Quite so," he said. "A lot of people promise. It's easy to promise. Quite a number of young men promise to marry the girl but they don't. Too many temptations, you see. I dare say you are worth helping. I'll grant you that. We can't really afford to write off really promising young players because they've slipped up, if we can avoid it. But we're cleaning up sport. And we've got to be sure, quite sure that it'll never happen again." "I'll give you my word," I said. "Yes, you've said that before. But I've only met you once. How are we to know that you'll keep it?" "What can I do to make you believe me?" I said. "You can give us security for your good behaviour," he said. I asked him what he meant. "I mean what I say," he said. "Security for your good behaviour in future. Mind you, I don't say my committee will accept it. As I said, I'm only one of them. But it's like bail. The magistrate wants something to ensure the prisoner will turn up. We want something to ensure you won't let us down." I asked what he meant by something. "Say three thousand pounds," he said. "What!" I said. "Don't get excited. You'll get it all back," he said. "We just want it as security. How old are you?" I told him. "Right," he said. "We want it for ten years. If you keep your fingers clean for ten years you'll get your three thousand back with five per cent interest." I told him I hadn't got three thousand shillings, let alone three thousand pounds. "Of course you haven't," he said, "but your father has. If he wants you to play at Wimbledon, he'll cough up." '

'Well,' said Stokes as the boy did not continue with his narrative, 'what happened then?'

'I was so taken aback, I didn't know what to say. I just said nothing. After a bit the man went on: "Well, what shall I say to my committee? That we shall just have to report you or that you'll promise to keep to the rules in future and that you'll give security for doing so?" "I'll promise to keep to the rules," I said. "What about security?" he asked. "My father would never agree," I said. "Well, that's tough on you," he said. "He ought to see you through. It's his own fault really, I expect. Not giving you enough pocket money, I mean. That was the cause of it, wasn't it?" "Yes, I suppose it was," I said. "Well," he said, "why not ask your father? No harm in asking." "He'd have a fit," I said. "He'll have two fits when you can't play at Wimbledon or scull at Henley," he said. "All right," I said,

"I'll ask him but I don't suppose for a moment he'll do it."
"Let's leave it at that," he said. "Meet me again here on
Thursday at two o'clock." "Why don't you come and see
my father yourself?" I asked. "You'd explain it better to
him than I would." "OK, he said, I'll do just that. Is he at
home now? I'll come back with you." We went back, but
my father wasn't in and he arranged to call next morning.'

'Can you describe this man?' asked Stokes.

'He was about thirty-five, I should think, and of
middling height.'

'Had he a moustache or beard or was he clean-shaven?'

'Clean-shaven.'

'Colour of his hair?'

'Brownish.'

'Did you ever see him again?'

'No, he never came the next morning. My father had got
on to the police and – '

But Stokes interrupted.

'You mustn't tell us what your father said to someone
else,' he said. Here was an example of a witness, who had
sworn to tell the whole truth, not being allowed to fulfil
his oath.

Stokes sat down and Ledbury was invited to cross-
examine.

'Mr Bentley,' he began, 'you've never seen me before any
more than Mr Bridges had, have you?'

'Except at the police court, no.'

'And, like Mr Bridges, you have no reason to believe that
I've anything to do with the case except that you see me in
the dock, have you?'

'Well, I've been told – ' began the boy, but the judge
intervened.

'You mustn't tell us what someone told you,' he said.

'But I can't answer the question without doing so,' said the boy.

'Mr Ledbury,' said the judge. 'Would you like the witness to say what he was told? I won't exclude the evidence if *you* want it in.'

'Would you, if you were in my position, my lord?'

'Don't be impertinent.'

'I don't intend to be, my lord, but I've always thought that, when a man appeared in person, the judge would usually steer him through the legal technicalities.'

'You know very well, Mr Ledbury,' said the judge, 'that, if you'd wanted to be represented, you could have been assisted by solicitors and counsel of the highest standing. You have ample means with which to engage them.'

'Quite so, my lord,' said Ledbury, 'but I've always understood that you only needed representation when you're guilty. If you're innocent, it's much better to do it yourself.'

'That is nonsense and you know it,' said the judge. 'However innocent you may be, you will nearly always be better off if you are represented by experienced counsel. That is why free legal aid was introduced, so that every accused person could be represented, even if he hadn't the means to employ a lawyer himself.'

'So you always get experienced counsel with free legal aid then?' said Ledbury. 'That's good hearing.'

'Don't be impudent,' said the judge. 'Kindly continue your cross-examination or sit down.'

'But I'm not sure how to answer your lordship's question and I asked your lordship for guidance.'

'You have elected to defend yourself. You must decide the matter for yourself. If you choose to ask the witness what he was told, I shall direct him to answer it.'

'Well, I'll ask you this, young man,' said Ledbury. 'Apart – '

'Call the witness by his proper name,' said the judge.

'I'm sorry, Mr Bentley,' said Ledbury. 'Apart from what anyone may have told you or what you may have read in the newspapers, have you any reason to think that I was anything to do with the League against Shamateurs?'

'Well, it sounds rather like the Association for the Protection of the Public from Fraud which Mr Bridges mentioned to me.'

'Of course it does,' said Ledbury, 'and it's obvious that someone is running a racket but why pick on me?'

'I was certainly surprised,' said the boy, 'when they said it was you.'

'When who said it was me?'

'The other witnesses.'

'What witnesses?'

'Miss Vane and the superintendent.'

'Well, forget what you heard them say.'

'I can't.'

'Suppose you hadn't heard their evidence, would you have thought that I had anything to do with your League or Mr Bridges' Association?'

'No, I don't think I should.'

'You don't *think*? Why aren't you sure that you wouldn't have suspected me?'

'Well, I am sure.'

'Good.'

'But after what I heard,' went on the boy before he could be stopped, 'I felt sure it was you.'

'Members of the jury,' said the judge. 'You will kindly disregard that answer. The only people who are concerned with the prisoner's guilt or innocence are you yourselves.

What this young man – what Mr Bentley thinks or feels sure about is totally beside the point.'

'Now, Mr Bentley,' went on Ledbury, 'did this man ever give you a name?'

'Yes, Simpson.'

'How did he come to give it?'

'When we went back home I asked him for it, so that I could introduce him to my father.'

'He apparently smelled a rat and didn't come?'

'I suppose so.'

'Did you think that you were being blackmailed?'

'No, I didn't. I thought that what the man said was true and that I would be reported unless I gave security.'

'That may be. But did you think it was a genuine society?'

'Yes, I did, or I wouldn't have taken the man back to father.'

'Your father spoke to the police?'

'Yes.'

'And, if the man had come, the police would have heard what he had to say?'

'Yes.'

'But he didn't come and that's the last you heard of it?'

'He didn't come, but it's not the last I heard of it.'

'What happened then?'

'I was reported to the authorities.'

'By whom?'

'Mr Simpson, I suppose.'

'So you haven't been able to play at Wimbledon or row at Henley?'

'No, I haven't. They were very sorry for me but held that I was disqualified.'

'Well, you were disqualified, weren't you?'

'Yes, technically, I was.'

'What's technical about it? You took money for coaching?'

'Yes.'

'You knew it was against the rules?'

'Yes.'

'And so you tried to keep it quiet.'

'There was nothing to keep quiet. I only did it for friends.'

'But you wouldn't have liked any of them to speak to the authorities about you?'

'They wouldn't have done so. I tell you, they were friends.'

'Did they know you weren't supposed to take money for it?'

'Yes, I told them so. At first I hadn't taken any money for it, but I was tempted when I was hard up.'

'Like the office boy who steals from the petty cash.'

'There was nothing dishonest about it.'

'Wasn't there?' asked Ledbury. 'When you apply to go in for a tournament don't you have to declare that you're an amateur within the meaning of the rules?'

'Yes.'

'But you weren't?'

'Not strictly, no.'

'But you were prepared to say you were?'

'Yes, I suppose so.'

'Although you knew you weren't.'

'Yes.'

'That would be telling a lie, wouldn't it?'

'Yes.'

'So you are prepared to tell a lie?'

'Everyone does sometimes.'

'Be careful, Mr Bentley,' said Ledbury, 'or you'll be in trouble with his lordship.'

'Don't try to be funny,' said the judge.

'Well, at any rate you were prepared to tell a lie in order to compete at the games you love?'

'I've already said so.'

'And I suppose you have in your life told other lies?'

'I expect so.'

'Well, how are the jury to know that you're not telling lies now?'

'I'm on oath.'

'Then you need an oath to make you tell the truth?'

'Certainly not.'

'You were prepared to tell a lie to get something you wanted in the sporting world?'

'I've admitted it.'

'So you are prepared to lie to get something you want?'

'Not necessarily.'

'If you want it badly enough?'

'I'm not always telling lies.'

'No one says you are. But, if you want a thing badly enough, you'd lie to get it.'

'No, I wouldn't.'

'Well, we know of one case when you would. So you can't say you wouldn't. You might lie to get it, mightn't you?'

'I suppose I might but it all depends on what it was.'

'How badly you wanted it, I suppose?'

'Perhaps.'

'You're giving evidence in this case for the prosecution?'

'Yes.'

'Do you want the prosecution to succeed?'

'It's nothing to do with me.'

'You have a mind and a will of your own. The prosecution isn't in your hands, of course. We all know that. But do you want it to succeed?'

'Yes, I do.'

'Why?'

'Because blackmail is a terrible crime.'

'And that's why you'd like me to be convicted?'

'Yes, if you're guilty.'

'But you think I'm guilty?'

'Yes, I do.'

'Then you want me to be convicted and when you want something you're prepared to lie to get it. Thank you, Mr Bentley.'

And Ledbury sat down.

'Just two questions, Mr Bentley,' said Stokes. 'Have you ever taken an oath before?'

'No.'

'Have you said anything today which you do not believe to be perfectly true?'

'No, I haven't.'

'Thank you, Mr Bentley,' said Stokes. 'Call Miss Vane, please.'

CHAPTER NINE

Margaret Vane

Margaret Vane had arrived at the court in time but only just. It is hard luck on witnesses, who have to come to court on pain of fine or imprisonment and then sometimes have to wait hours before they are called into the witness box. On the other hand, the courts could not function properly unless witnesses were compelled to attend court (unless ill) in plenty of time to be available to give their evidence.

The reason that Margaret was nearly late was because she had been at the hospital where the man who had been injured when the car charged at her was still detained. She hated to leave him and on this occasion stayed too long.

She went into the witness box and took the oath.

'Miss Vane,' began Stokes, 'you may be in the witness box a long time. I'm sure his lordship would let you sit down if you wanted.'

'Thank you. I'd prefer to stand for the moment.'

'Is your name Margaret Vane and do you live at – '

But Margaret interrupted.

'May I write my address down, please, my lord?' she asked.

'Certainly,' said the judge.

'Am I allowed to see it?' asked Ledbury.

'Is it relevant to the case?'

'How can I tell without seeing it?'

'If it becomes necessary for the purposes of your defence,' said the judge, 'you shall certainly see it.'

'Thank you, my lord. It's nice to know that an accused person *may* be allowed to see the evidence on which he is being tried.'

'Unless it is relevant the jury won't see it or hear it.'

'If it isn't relevant, my lord,' asked Ledbury, 'why is she asked the question at all?'

'It is desirable that the name and address of every witness shall be recorded. For one thing it might be necessary to get in touch with them again.'

'All right. Forget the address. I don't want to see it.'

'If you don't behave yourself I shall fine you for contempt of court,' said the judge.

'I'm sorry, my lord,' said Ledbury. 'Please ascribe my misbehaviour to over-anxiety. It's a new and very unpleasant experience being in the dock.'

'Let's get on, Mr Stokes,' said the judge. 'Is this your address, Miss Vane?' he continued, looking at the piece of paper on which Margaret had written it.

'Yes, my lord.'

'Very well then. Yes, Mr Stokes?'

'Miss Vane,' said Stokes, 'what are you?'

'At the moment, d'you mean?' asked Margaret.

'Very well, at the moment.'

'I can only describe myself as a hunted woman.'

'I beg your pardon?' said Stokes.

'A hunted woman. Two attempts have been made either to kidnap or murder me. I'm under constant police protection. Even at this moment. I like policemen very much but, as the Duke in *Patience* said, toffee for breakfast, toffee for dinner – '

'Miss Vane,' said the judge, 'please confine yourself to answering the questions.'

'I'm sorry, my lord, but I want you and the public to know my position. I'm less free than the man in the dock and in constant danger.'

'Are you suggesting that your situation is anything to do with the accused?'

'Of course I am, my lord. If he can get rid of me, he's a free man. This man and the people in his employ will stop at nothing. They have the money and the power. They'd even get at you, my lord, if they thought it would do any good.'

During this outburst the judge tried several times to stop Margaret from going on but he was unsuccessful.

'This is very unfortunate, Mr Stokes,' he said when Margaret stopped. 'Are you going to produce any evidence that the accused is directly or indirectly responsible for what the witness says has happened to her?'

'Frankly, no, my lord.'

'Then it should never have been stated to the jury. Mr Ledbury, do you ask for a new trial before another jury?'

'No, my lord, thank you,' said Ledbury. 'This young woman's little outburst doesn't disturb me in the least. Nor will it worry you, my lord, or the jury when you've heard a bit more about her. She'll use every card in the pack. Fortunately I've got all the aces.'

'No doubt you took them out in advance,' said Margaret.

'Don't, please, Miss Vane.'

'My lord,' said Ledbury, 'one thing I think you and the jury ought to know before you go on with the case.'

'What is it?'

'This woman has been a professional actress.'

'Is that correct?'

'Yes, my lord,' said Margaret.

'Well, we don't want any histrionics here, please,' said the judge.

'Thank you, my lord,' said Ledbury. 'So much for the hunted woman, members of the jury.'

'Go on, please, Mr Stokes,' said the judge.

'Have you any job at the moment, Miss Vane?'

'Only keeping out of harm's way.'

'When were you on the stage?'

'When I was twenty. For five years. I finished about six years ago.'

'And since then?'

'I took a secretarial course. Then I had various jobs.'

'Did you eventually have a post with a man who, with his lordship's permission, I'll call Mr X, a well-known journalist?'

But Ledbury intervened before Margaret could answer. 'Why should his lordship permit it?' he asked angrily. 'Am I to be the only person in this case to appear in my own name? This witness' name isn't Vane at all. Now we have her employer, who's to be called Mr X. Does the usher want to be called Mr Y?'

There was a titter of laughter in court which the usher immediately suppressed.

'You won't help yourself by being facetious,' said the judge. 'It is quite normal in these cases for names to be withheld. If it becomes in the interests of justice for his name to be disclosed I shall see that this is done. Did Mr X employ you, Miss Vane?'

'Yes.'

'Very well, Mr Stokes,' said the judge. 'Please continue.'

'Was it your employment with Mr X,' asked Stokes, 'that brought you into contact with this case?'

'Yes.'

'So that there may be no doubt about the matter,' went on Stokes, 'did Mr X himself do anything discreditable?'

'Certainly not. He is a most honourable man.'

'Why is Mr X not being called, Mr Stokes?' asked the judge.

'For one thing he is at the moment seriously ill in hospital as the result of a – as the result of an accident – '

'Accident!!' said Margaret.

'Don't interrupt, please,' said the judge.

'For another,' continued Stokes, 'I very much doubt if there is any admissible evidence which he could give.'

'Very well,' said the judge. 'Go on, please.'

'Go on, please, Miss Vane,' said Stokes. 'Tell my lord and the jury what happened.'

'Mr X wanted to find out who was behind all these blackmail cases and he asked me if I'd help. I said I would.'

'What was the plan of campaign?'

'It was necessary to get someone into the organisation.'

'How did you proceed?'

'Mr X sent someone to offer information about me to a person he'd discovered to be one of the gang. In due course I was approached and threatened with exposure. Instead of agreeing to pay money I offered to provide information about various people.'

'What people?'

'Mr X gave me the names.'

'What happened?'

'I'm afraid some of them were blackmailed.'

'You mean they actually paid to avoid exposure?'

'Yes.'

'So Mr X was able to give genuine information?'

'Certainly. Most of us know something discreditable about someone else. But an experienced journalist must know more than most people.'

'Go on.'

'Well, I started to become very valuable to the organisation, and eventually I became important enough to meet Mr Jones. He was responsible for the collection of information. I also met Nottingham, who collected the money.'

'What did Mr Jones look like?'

'He was middle-aged – about 45 – slightly bald – as a matter of fact he looked a little like that juryman in the front row – furthest away from me.'

The juryman coloured and shifted uneasily. The other jurors looked at him.

'It isn't him, I suppose?' asked Stokes.

'Oh – no. There's only a slight resemblance.'

'Could you identify Mr Jones if you saw him?'

'Oh – certainly.'

'How often did you meet him?'

'At first only occasionally – but in the last two or three months many times.'

'Were you paid for what you did?'

'At first not. But, when they saw how useful I was, they began to pay me. it wasn't a specific wage. But from time to time I was given a lump sum – anything from twenty to fifty pounds.'

'What was the total?'

'Several hundred pounds.'

'Why didn't you go to the police about Mr Jones?'

'Because Mr X wanted me to find out who was behind it all and he felt sure that, if we went to the police about Mr Jones, we'd never get the real head.'

'Did you ever meet the accused?'

'Yes. Once.'

'Tell my lord and the jury the circumstances.'

'I'd got to know Mr Jones pretty well and one day I told him that I'd got information about a Cabinet Minister. He became very excited about this and asked me a lot of questions. In fact what I told him was quite untrue. Mr X had invented it. Eventually Mr Jones said he wanted me to tell the story to someone else. He referred to him as Mr Bennett but in fact it was the accused. I was introduced to him by Mr Jones in Hyde Park.'

'On what day?'

'On the 11th June of this year.'

'Are you sure it was the accused?'

'Perfectly. I've already picked him out in an identification parade.'

'Tell us the conversation between you and the accused.'

'For a long time he talked about other subjects – cricket, politics, clothes and so on. Then he suddenly asked me if I knew this Cabinet Minister. I said, no, not personally. He then put to me the information which I'd given to Mr Jones.'

'What was it?'

'That he'd been selling Cabinet secrets to a journalist.'

'What did the accused say about it?'

'He wanted chapter and verse. Mr X had given me two examples of information which one newspaper published before all the others. In point of fact there was nothing sinister about them. The one newspaper had just got in first. But it was consistent with the information having been improperly obtained, and, as all the other things I'd told Mr Jones had turned out to be true, the accused believed me.'

'What did he say?'

'That we'd make a killing. Mr X had particularly chosen a Minister who was known to be very wealthy. The accused said we ought to be able to get enough to close down. He said he was a little disturbed by all the prosecutions which had taken place. He mentioned a bank clerk and a parson. He was also a bit worried about an undergraduate who gave tennis lessons. No one had been caught but the boy's father had gone to the police. So far no one had suspected him but he didn't believe in riding his luck too long. He'd take £100,000 off this man and call it a day. I was to have £5,000. He said that so many people failed because they were too greedy. The great thing was not to ask more than a man could give. He said it was a pity they'd squeezed Mr Bridges for £3 a week. If they'd made it £2 he'd have been paying still.'

'Who mentioned Mr Bridges?'

'He did.'

'By name?'

'Yes.'

'Did he know all about the case?'

'Oh, yes. He even said that he'd no sympathy with what he called desiccated gentlemen.'

'You say he mentioned other cases?'

'Yes, several. He made it quite plain that he was the organiser of the whole business.'

'Why did he tell you all this?'

'I was important to him for the final case of the Cabinet Minister and he reckoned I must be quite safe as I was so completely involved in other cases.'

'Thank you, Miss Vane.'

'Mr Ledbury,' said the judge, 'would you like to cross-examine?'

'Yes, please,' said Ledbury, standing up, 'I would. Now – Miss Vane – it was Vane, wasn't it?'

'Yes.'

'We'll come back to that in a moment. Would you like to sit down before I begin?'

'No, thank you.'

'A glass of water?'

'I will not tolerate this,' said the judge. 'Your right is to question the witness, not to threaten or taunt her.'

'I was merely being civil, my lord. In fact Mr Stokes offered her a seat. Why shouldn't I?'

'Proceed with your cross-examination or sit down.'

'Now, Miss Vane – if that is your real name – you're telling lies because you hate me, aren't you?'

'That's two questions,' said the judge.

'I've many more to ask than that,' said Ledbury.

'No doubt,' said the judge, 'but you must ask them one at a time. Have you stopped beating your wife?'

'I beg your pardon?' said Ledbury.

'That,' said the judge, 'is the classical instance of a double and therefore unfair question. How is a man who has never beaten his wife to answer it? If he says "yes" it implies that he used to beat his wife. If he says "no" it means that he's still beating her. So first of all you must ask him if he has ever beaten his wife. That he can answer.'

'I see,' said Ledbury. 'Thank you, my lord. I must think for a moment how to put it.'

'There's no real difficulty about it,' said the judge. 'You are entitled first to suggest to her that she is telling lies and then to suggest a reason why she should tell lies.'

'Thank you, my lord,' said Ledbury, and looking straight at Margaret he said: 'You are telling lies, aren't you?'

'Certainly not,' said Margaret.

'Well, you do hate me, don't you?'

There was a pause and then: 'Yes, I do,' said Margaret.

'Quite so,' said Ledbury. 'You don't hate Mr X, do you?'

'Certainly not.'

'Quite the contrary, you might say.'

'I don't know what you mean. Is this anything to do with the case, my lord?'

'I don't know,' said the judge. 'It may be.'

'It certainly is. Do you love Mr X as much as you hate me? I'm sorry, my lord. Have I stopped beating my wife? You're in love with Mr X, aren't you?'

'That's nothing to do with the case.'

'He wants to see me convicted, doesn't he?'

Margaret remained silent.

'Well?' continued Ledbury.

'Yes, if he lives, he'd like to see you convicted.'

'And I'll tell you why. If I'm convicted he can pretty well write what he likes about me and make a packet. If I'm acquitted, he won't even recoup what he's paid you.'

'That's nothing to do with it.'

'I'd have thought it was a great deal to do with it. You think I'm responsible for his injuries, don't you?'

'Yes, I do,' said Margaret. 'And it's no thanks to you that he's improving. You meant to kill me but you nearly killed him.'

As the judge seemed about to intervene, Ledbury looked towards him and said: 'It's quite all right, my lord. I want this evidence.' Then, turning to Margaret, he went on: 'It's not surprising, then, that you're giving evidence against me. I'd feel the same in your position. Only you've made a mistake. That unfortunate accident was nothing to do with me.'

'Accident!' said Margaret bitterly.

'Let's say it was deliberate,' said Ledbury. 'You think I nearly killed your boy friend. You'd feel differently about me if you knew I had nothing to do with it.'

'It was you I met in the park,' said Margaret, 'if that's what you're getting at.'

'But it was dusk. How can you be sure?'

'I saw your face clearly enough. We were together for over half an hour.'

'Now tell me something else. Your real name isn't Vane, is it?'

'Have I got to answer, my lord?'

'Why shouldn't you?' asked the judge.

'Because the accused – if he gets off – or, if he doesn't, his brother, or one of his henchmen – may make things very uncomfortable for my relatives. I was a spy and spies have to be discouraged.'

'When did you change your name?' asked the judge.

'When I agreed to help Mr X.'

'What does her name matter, Mr Ledbury?'

'I propose to show that this woman is a liar,' said Ledbury.

'Well?'

'If she has convictions registered against her, I'm entitled to refer to them, am I not?'

'Certainly.'

'How can I tell if Miss Vane has – for example, been convicted of perjury – if the conviction was under the name of, say, Smith?'

'Miss Vane,' said the judge, 'have you been convicted of perjury under any name?'

'Certainly not.'

'Have you been convicted of any criminal offence under any name?'

'Never, my lord.'

'Not even a parking offence?' asked Ledbury.

'Well – yes, I have.'

'What about a customs offence?' he continued. 'Trying to get a camera through?'

'May I explain?'

'I'd prefer you to answer the question,' said Ledbury. 'Were you not convicted of trying to get a camera through the customs undeclared?'

'Yes, I was.'

'Don't you know that's a criminal offence?'

'Yes – I suppose I do, but – '

'But you swore to the jury that you'd never been convicted of any offence. That wasn't true, was it?'

'Not strictly – but I only tried to smuggle the camera through in order to get in touch with you.'

'Really! That wasn't very bright. .Who worries about customs offences?'

'Do you mean by that, Mr Ledbury,' said the judge, 'that you don't think anyone would try to blackmail a person simply because of a customs offence?'

'Am I supposed to be cross-examining the witness, my lord, or are you cross-examining me?' asked Ledbury.

The judge thought for a moment or two and, realising that he was in the wrong, he said: 'You needn't answer my question. Proceed with your cross-examination.'

'Thank you very much. It's lucky I'm able to stand up for myself, members of the jury. Now, Miss Vane – or Miss Smith or whatever you'd like to be called – what do you know about my brother?'

'Only what you told me.'

'You've never met him?'

'No.'

'Unless, of course, it was my brother you met in the park.'

'It wasn't.'

'How d'you know?'

'Because I recognise you. He's not a twin, as far as I know.'

'How d'you know he's not a twin?' asked Ledbury.

'Well, of course, I don't for certain,' said Margaret.

'Well then, mightn't it have been a twin brother of mine?'

'If you have a twin brother exactly like you, I suppose it might,' said Margaret. 'But I don't believe your brother is a twin.'

'Why shouldn't he be?'

'Mr Ledbury,' intervened the judge, 'in due course you will be entitled to prove that you have a twin brother and furthermore you will also be entitled to call him. Do you wish to give evidence that it was he who met Miss Vane in the park?'

'But, my lord,' said Ledbury, 'I don't suppose he'd want to come to court. And, anyway, isn't it for the prosecution to prove I haven't a twin brother?'

'Certainly not,' said the judge, 'the witness says she recognises you as the man she met in the park. She may be lying or mistaken but, if the mistake is due to your having a twin brother, it is for you to prove it.'

'My lord,' intervened Stokes, 'if Mr Ledbury states that he has a twin brother I will immediately take steps to have it confirmed.'

'Well, I haven't, as a matter of fact,' said Ledbury, 'but I just wanted to test the witness, to see how sure she was. She certainly never met me in the park.'

'Don't address the jury, please,' said the judge. 'Continue with your cross-examination.'

'Miss Vane,' said Ledbury. 'I have here a good deal of information about you.' He brought out a file of papers. 'And I'm going to ask you a lot of awkward questions about it.'

'Ask your questions but don't threaten the witness,' said the judge.

'My lord, I was not threatening the witness. I wanted to explain to the jury – '

'Ask your questions. Don't make statements.'

'It is only fair that I should be allowed to explain to the jury how I'm able to ask my next questions. Otherwise they might think my knowledge of the accused showed that I was the man concerned.'

'Ask your questions,' repeated the judge.

'I have obtained the information on which the questions are based for the purposes of this case. Now, Miss Vane, did you know a man called Temple?'

'Yes, I did.'

'Was he a churchwarden?'

'Yes.'

'Did he go in for football pools?'

'He did.'

'Without much success?'

'Not as far as I know.'

'Did he eventually try to achieve success?'

'What do you mean?'

'You know quite well what I mean. Did he put in a false claim and was it investigated and found to be false and did the pools promoters refuse to pay?'

'That is so.'

'But he wasn't prosecuted.'

'Not as far as I know.'

'Did you go to this man Temple and tell him that he was going to be prosecuted?'

'No – I didn't.'

'Did someone else to your knowledge go to him and say this?'

'I believe so.'

'Did you later visit him and say that you might be able to prevent a prosecution?'

'Yes – I did.'

'Was that true? Could you have prevented a prosecution?'

'No, I couldn't have.'

'So you told him a lie?'

'Yes.'

'In order to frighten him into paying money?'

'Yes.'

'And did you for some months collect money regularly from him under the pretence that you had to pay other people to prevent the prosecution?'

'It wasn't entirely a pretence. I did have to pay. I had to pay you.'

'That is an absolute lie. You've never paid me a penny.'

'Not directly – but I paid direct to Mr Nottingham who paid it to you.'

'How do you know? Did you ever see him do it?'

'Of course not, but in our talk in the park you made it plain that you were the person behind the whole thing. You were rather proud of it.'

'We'll come to this so-called interview later on. At the moment I'm asking you about your own blackmailing activities. Do you agree that you obtained substantial sums of money from Mr Temple?'

'Yes.'

'And part of it you kept for yourself?'

'I was paid a commission or whatever you call it. At first I had it from a man whose name I didn't know, but later I got it from Nottingham.'

'How many people altogether did you blackmail?'

'Seven or eight, I suppose.'

'Have *you* ever been prosecuted for blackmail?'

'No.'

'Why not?'

'Because although they *thought* I was extorting money from them, I wasn't really. I knew it would all be repaid to them, as it was.'

'By whom?'

'By one of the newspapers to which Mr X contributes.'

'So you frighten a person out of his wits and then give him back his money and say it makes it all right. Did any of your customers commit suicide?'

'No.'

'They might have.'

'Anyone *might* commit suicide.'

'We know that. But your threats might have made a churchwarden, for example, take his own life. How would he relish reading the Lessons or taking the collection with the knowledge that at any moment all his pretended piety might be blown sky-high? Did not you and Mr X gamble with other people's lives, if what you say is true?'

'We took a risk. We had to. There appeared to be no other way of finding out who you were. All right, we did risk the lives of a few people so that hundreds or thousands of others might be saved.'

'Guinea-pigs.'

'What is Mr Ledbury asking?' put in Stokes.

'Yes, Mr Ledbury,' said the judge, 'what is the question?'

'They used human guinea-pigs, my lord. Well, didn't you?'

'We did what we had to.'

'Are you proud of your behaviour?'

'I'm neither proud nor ashamed. It was dirty work, if you like, but I did it to prevent dirtier.'

'I suggest that you did it entirely for your own purposes and your own gain. And, no doubt, that of Mr X as well.'

'That is absolutely untrue.'

'We'll see about that. First let's see where we've got to at present. You are the chief witness for the prosecution?'

'That's a matter for me,' said Stokes.

'Let's put it like this, then, Miss Vane. You are the only person who claims to be able to say anything about me.'

'I believe so.'

'And you yourself are a persistent blackmailer?'

'I behaved like one for a very good reason but I am not one.'

'You are also a liar. You said you'd never been convicted of crime and you had been.'

'My so-called crime was committed for the same purpose.'

'You don't mind soiling your hands?'

'I agreed it was dirty work.'

'What would you stop at? Murder?'

'That's ridiculous.'

'Is it? Didn't you realise that a person who's blackmailed may commit suicide in desperation?'

'They were told the truth as soon as we could.'

'Why not at the time?'

'Because we had to be sure that your investigators would believe it. The people concerned weren't actors.'

'Like you,' put in Ledbury.

'Unless they really believed they were being blackmailed,' Margaret went on, 'they might very well have given the game away.'

'A charming game – which you were playing with other people's lives.'

'You've made your point,' said the judge. 'Kindly continue to ask questions.'

'You didn't hate the people you blackmailed, did you?'

'Certainly not.'

111

'But you blackmailed them just the same. I wonder what you'd do to someone you hated.'

At that moment the judge's clerk came in from the door behind the Bench and handed an envelope to the judge.

'This has just arrived for you, sir,' he whispered to the judge. 'The messenger said it was vitally urgent.'

The judge opened the envelope and read the contents. As he did so he went white. After a moment or two he whispered to his clerk.

'Go and ring up my house at once and see if Angela is still at home. If not, ask where she's gone. Come back and give me the answer. Be as quick as you can.'

The clerk left and the judge looked again at the note. He felt sick. For the first time in his life he did not know what to do.

CHAPTER TEN

An Interview

By a supreme effort the judge managed after about half a minute to let the proceedings continue and to concentrate on them. Those who complain at the long holidays which judges enjoy do not appreciate the strain on the human mechanism which continuous concentration for prolonged periods entails. A judge should (and nearly always does) listen to every word which is spoken in court, whether by a witness or an advocate. In the normal way he does this from 10.30 a.m. to 4.15 p.m. with an interval of anything up to an hour for lunch in the middle. In addition to this task of concentration a judge should be (and often is) extremely patient with all who come in front of him. In order that he may be in a physical and mental condition to discharge these twin duties of concentration and patience really satisfactorily, it is important that he should have long periods of rest between the sittings of the courts. Of course judges could continue to discharge their duties reasonably if they had three weeks' holiday instead of thirteen. Of course there are judges who would still be impatient if they had thirty weeks' holiday in the year. But, if the public wants to have as a general rule judges who will give the best possible service which human beings can give, they must give them long holidays. Most people probably think that justice is such a precious commodity that every reasonable step should be taken to arrive at it. A long holiday for the judges is one of the steps. Take away the holidays and you will still have justice but (to adopt the *Good Food Guide*'s nomenclature) it will be Class B justice instead of Class C, and what is wanted ideally is Class C with a crown.

It is a pity that judges cannot have labels, like hotels, with 'recommended by so-and-so' etc., etc. If the idea appeals to the publishers of the *Law List* (or some less reverential body) they might compile each year a list of all the judges with all their virtues and imperfections shortly described. And perhaps one year a Class B judge would be promoted to Class C. How would this do? 'It is worth a detour off the Strand to see Mr Justice Grain at work. Good simple judgments. Friendly and comfortable. But the service is a little erratic. Class B, sometimes Class C.'

The only objection to such a compilation is that the litigant would normally be unable to use it for the purpose of choosing his judge, as the traveller chooses his hotel. Moreover, just as a hotel guest will go ruefully into a hotel which has been castigated by Mr Cyril Ray or Mr Quentin Crewe but which is the only one available at the time, so a litigant would not be very happy when his case was opened before a Class A judge of whom Mr XYZ had written: 'This judge is charming enough but he is so anxious to please both parties that he can never make up his mind which way to decide the issue. The toss of a coin would have been a cheaper method of ending the case.'

Mr Justice Hereford managed to listen to the evidence which followed, but lurking at the back of his mind was a terrible fear, a fear which was confirmed when his clerk came back five minutes later and told him that Angela was no longer at home. A uniformed chauffeur had called for her with a message apparently (though not in fact) coming from the judge.

He looked at the clock.

'It's nearly four o'clock,' he said. 'I think I'll adjourn now. Members of the jury, please be back in your places punctually on Monday.'

He rose and went to his room followed by his clerk.

'What is it, sir?' asked the clerk. 'What's happened?'

'I must think,' said the judge.

'Has anything happened to Miss Angela?' asked the clerk anxiously.

'Don't ask questions, please,' said the judge almost irritably. 'No, don't go away,' he said, as he saw his clerk going towards the door. 'I'm sorry I'm a bit irritable. I've got to think.'

He looked at the letter which he had received. It was typewritten on a plain sheet of paper with no address and no signature on it. It said: 'We hold your daughter. If you wish to see her again, give an interview to a Mr Cartwright who will call on you shortly after you receive this note. If you communicate with the police or tell anyone else about this note you will never see your daughter again. This will also be the case if Mr Cartwright is not allowed to leave the building without being followed.'

'John,' said the judge eventually, 'I'm expecting a visitor, a Mr Cartwright. Let them know downstairs. I want him sent up at once.'

'Very good, sir,' said the clerk, 'but – '

'Now no "buts", John, there's a good fellow.'

'Very good, sir,' said the clerk and went towards the door.

'Just one other thing,' said the judge. 'I want you to remain outside the door during the interview. Don't try to listen to what's said but – '

'Sir, I wouldn't dream of – '

'Do wait till I've finished,' said the judge. 'Of course I know you wouldn't listen but you might have thought something was the matter.'

'Well, I do,' said the clerk.

'Then keep it to yourself.'

'Have you been threatened, sir? Shall I go to the police?'

'In no circumstances are you to go for the police. You must trust me to know what is best. Do just what I say. Show the man in and stay outside within earshot.'

'I don't like it, sir,' said the clerk.

'Nor do I, John,' said the judge, 'but, if our association over the years means anything to you, you will do just what I say and mention the matter to no one. No one,' he repeated.

'Very good, sir.'

At that moment the telephone rang.

'If that's Mr Cartwright tell them to send him up and remember what I said.'

Five minutes later the clerk showed a man into the judge's room.

'Mr Cartwright, sir,' he said and went out and waited. The man walked into the room slowly and, before saying anything, wandered round it.

'It's not bugged if that's what you're looking for,' said the judge.

'No,' said the man, 'you haven't had the time, for one thing. For another, as you've agreed to see me, I expect you're going to be sensible.'

He continued to walk round the room for a short time. 'This isn't much of a place to give a judge. You should see my brother's office. It knocks spots off this. And he couldn't even fine a man forty shillings, let alone send him to prison for life.'

He took out a cigarette and lit it.

'Mind if I smoke?' he asked as he puffed at it.

'What do you want?' asked the judge, unable to keep urgency out of his voice.

'Easy does it,' said the man, 'there's no hurry.'

He sat down in an armchair.

'Mind if I sit down?' he asked.

'Where is Angela?' asked the judge.

'You seem anxious,' said the man. 'An only child, by any chance?'

The judge did not answer.

'Please answer my question,' said the man, 'or there's no point in my staying. And, if I go away without our business being concluded, I'm afraid it'll be a question not whether Angela *is* an only child but whether she *was* one.'

'She is an only child.'

'Good. Well, one good turn deserves another. My name's not Cartwright. Like to know what it is?'

As the judge said nothing, the man got up.

'Now, look here,' he said, 'in that court you've just left you may be the king-pin, but at this interview I am. And I warn you that, if I have any more nonsense from you, I shall simply leave and that'll be the end of your only child. Make no mistake about it. Either you answer my questions and do what I say or else. Ring the bell and have me arrested if you like. But the ring of the bell will be your child's death-knell. We haven't abolished the death penalty in our profession, whatever you may have done in yours.'

'You're blackguards – you stop at nothing.'

'Mere abuse will get you nowhere. In point of fact, I won't have it. I'm in command here, not you. And you'll answer my questions as genially and politely as you expect your witnesses to do. Is that understood? Come along now, is that understood?'

'Yes.'

'Now do you want to know who I am?'

'Yes.'

'My name is Ledbury. George Ledbury. I'm Cliff's brother.'

'I see. What is it you want?'

'I'm asking the questions,' said George Ledbury. 'You speak when I want you to and not before.'

He smiled at the judge.

'What does it feel like to be at the receiving end? Come on, tell me. I want to know. It's interesting. You're so used to lording it over others, this must be a change for you. What does it feel like?'

'I am so distressed about my daughter that I can think of nothing else,' said the judge.

'Good. That's as it should be,' said George Ledbury. 'My note has apparently successfully started the softening-up process. I assume you told your clerk to telephone to see if it was just a hoax and found it was true enough.'

'How did you get her and where is she?'

'Now, now,' said George Ledbury, 'didn't I tell you that I was to ask the questions?'

'It's only natural I should want to know,' said the judge. 'You can't be all that inhuman.'

'But I am, my dear chap, quite as bad as that and worse. After all, if we don't mind disposing of the little girl herself, your mere feelings won't affect us very much, will they?'

'No, I suppose not.'

'Well, I'll tell you something you'll be pleased to hear. Angela is safe and sound.'

'Thank God.'

'No, judge, thank us. By the way, should I call you "judge" or what?'

'I don't mind what you call me.'

'Kindly answer the question. Should I call you "judge" or not?'

The judge had great difficulty in answering civilly but he could see that there was no alternative.

'In England only barristers call a High Court judge "Judge".'

'Well, what should I call you? Now don't say you don't mind. I want to know. What should I call you?'

'In court you would call me "my lord".'

'I know that. What should I call you here?'

'It depends in what capacity you come here. If you came on official business you would call me "my lord". If you came as a stranger about something else I suppose you would call me "Sir James". My name is James Hereford.'

'Yes, I got as far as that. Good. Now I know where I am. I shall call you "my lord". That means I'm on official business. You would call anything to do with a case official business, wouldn't you?'

'In the normal way, yes.'

'Well, although this is hardly the normal way, I've come to see you about my brother's case, my lord.'

The judge said nothing.

'Good, you're learning. Don't speak unless you're spoken to. I've just told you your little girl is alive and well. And happy. She doesn't know anything's wrong. It's up to you whether she stays that way. Would you like to speak to her?'

'Very much.'

'All right, you shall. But one false move and she'll have had it. In a moment get me an outside line. And don't watch what number I'm dialling. Tell your little girl you want her to go away for the weekend with some friends of yours. Say you'll join her if you can. But, if you can't, you'll see her on Monday. You needn't add "you hope". But it all depends on you whether you see her on Monday.'

He paused and the judge was about to speak.

'Now – now – you're slipping,' said George Ledbury playfully. 'Now you want to know what to do in order to get your little girl back, don't you?'

'I do.'

'Very natural. Very natural indeed. Well, we don't want any money. That'll be a relief for you, if you've been trying to see how much you can afford. Not a penny piece. That's decent of us, isn't it?'

'I would pay all I had,' said the judge, 'and promise that no attempt would be made to arrest or prosecute you.'

'Yes, I believe you would,' said George Ledbury, 'and, what's more, I think you'd keep your word. Your little girl means everything to you, doesn't she?'

'She does.'

'Fine. That's also as it should be. Now you want to know the vital question. What have you got to do? That's right, isn't it?'

'It is.'

'What a pleasant interview this is. We agree about everything. Well, it's perfectly simple. All you've got to do is to see that Cliff is acquitted.'

'Your brother, you mean?'

'Of course. Now get me an outside line.'

In a minute or so the judge was talking to Angela. He was greatly relieved to hear that she did not appear in the least frightened. She had accepted that her father wanted to give her a surprise. Apart altogether from the influence of the threats which had been made to him the judge had not the slightest wish to do other than what he had been told. It would be terrible for the girl to learn or suspect that she had been kidnapped. Everything he said was designed to prevent her from suspecting the truth. After they had been chatting for a few minutes George Ledbury held up his hand to indicate that the conversation must end. The judge told Angela that, if he didn't see her before, he'd see her on Monday.

'God bless you, darling,' he said as he put down the receiver.

'Apart from that last remark,' said George Ledbury, 'that was pretty good. You were sensible. You could see it was as much in your own interest as in mine to do what I told you. And now let's get down to business. Are there any questions you'd like to ask?'

'Questions?' For the moment the judge was puzzled.

'Yes, about how to get Cliff off.'

'But it's for the jury to try him, not me.'

'Be your age, chum,' said George Ledbury. 'Everyone knows the jury brings in the verdict. You don't have to have five A levels or a degree to know that. But the judge can steer them to the right verdict.'

'How d'you expect me to do that?'

'There you go again, chum, asking questions. But I'm glad I've interested you anyway. As I said, the situation is perfectly simple. As soon as Cliff's acquitted, your little girl will be returned to you in the same good condition as she was when we took her away. We don't put people down for fun. Only if there's a reason. So she comes back when Cliff comes out. But – *but*,' he emphasised, 'if I don't get clean away from here and if Cliff is convicted, you lose your little girl. That's certain and final.'

'You're asking me to break my judicial oath – to try cases without fear or favour.'

'That's right, chum, and you're going to break it.'

The judge remained silent.

'I suppose you think the oath you took imposes a responsibility on you.'

'Of course it does,' said the judge.

'Quite so, but doesn't being a father have its responsibilities? Incidentally this should be a lesson to old men not to have children. You must have been fifty-five at least when she was born.'

'I was fifty-six.'

'Well, it's too late to worry about that now. The short point is I'm not going to have my brother put away for forty or fifty years. That's what you'd give him, isn't it?'

'It's a very bad case if he's guilty. He'd certainly get a long sentence.'

'D'you think he'll be convicted?'

'Well,' began the judge, 'it partly depends on – '

'Now you can stop all that whereas-ing and legal humming and ha-ing. Tell me what you think. Is he likely to be convicted?'

'Yes, I think he is.'

'Could I do a deal with you on sentence? Would you promise to give him not more than six months?'

'People would think I'd gone mad,' said the judge.

'There's something in that,' said George Ledbury. 'That's one of the reasons I came to see you. The thing's got to appear all right. If people thought you'd gone off your head they might interfere before Cliff had been released. So I don't think the short sentence idea is very good. Forget it. I never did think much of it. No, you've got to get him off altogether.'

'Is he guilty?'

'What's that got to do with it?'

'Well, if he's not guilty, he'll be found not guilty. Even if he's guilty, the jury might have a doubt.'

'Well,' said George Ledbury, 'let's assume for the purpose of argument that he's guilty and that, the jury would have no doubt, what are you going to do?'

'You're asking me to do something that no judge in England has done for hundreds of years.'

'That should be a change for you, chum. It must be a bore always having to do what the other chaps have done before you. Besides, if you're worrying about that oath you took, you think of your responsibilities to your little girl. You didn't take an oath to protect her but, if fathers did take oaths to do that, you'd have taken one, wouldn't you?'

'Of course.'

'You've just as much a duty towards her as you have towards the law. Look, suppose you saw her run across a busy road and slip, you'd be after her to save her, wouldn't you?'

'Of course.'

'Although your doing so might cause an even worse accident. You'd only think about saving your little girl, wouldn't you?'

'I suppose I would.'

'All the others could go hang, so long as she was saved. That's right, isn't it?'

'I expect it is.'

'Well, this time it isn't people. No one else is going to be hurt. Just let the law go hang for once. After all you've upheld it for years. You won't be doing it for me or for my brother, but to save your daughter. And you've a duty to save your daughter.'

'I've a duty to comply with my oath too.'

'Quite so, but in a pinch which comes first? What right have you to condemn a little girl to death? Even if she weren't your own, you'd have a duty to save her. But, as she is yours, the duty is all the greater. You brought her into the world, you've no right to kick her out of it.'

'Suppose I agreed to do what you ask,' said the judge, 'it wouldn't be at all easy. I don't believe your brother's made at all a good impression on the jury. And, if he doesn't do better when he's giving evidence, the jury may very well convict him.'

'You're right there, chum. He's like me. Too cocky by half. Look at the way I'm talking to you. Disgraceful. I'm sure juries don't like that sort of thing.'

'So, whatever I did, he might be convicted. A jury's not bound to follow a judge's lead, however strongly he may give it.'

'You can get them to stop the case before Cliff has to give evidence. I've read of that, surely.'

'If there's no evidence against him, certainly. But here there is evidence.'

'What's the chief evidence against him? The girl, isn't it?'

'Yes.'

'Well, smash her to pieces.'

'How?'

'That's your province, chum, not mine. But you've got to do it so that it looks genuine. You've got to act the part all right. You've got to act as you've never acted before. Otherwise, if people thought you were off your rocker, they might interfere before the trial was over.'

'I still can't guarantee the result,' said the judge.

'Well, I can guarantee the result if you don't succeed,' said George Ledbury. 'One hundred per cent.'

After a short pause he added: 'You can always resign after Cliff's been acquitted. But not too soon. Not to make it too obvious. Though, come to think of it, we shall be out of the country. So it doesn't matter all that.'

Again there was silence. George Ledbury broke it.

'I've got it,' he said. 'If the jury don't believe that girl, Cliff's away, isn't he?'

'I should think so.'

'Now, if she refuses to answer a question, you can tell the jury that she's not a reliable witness, can't you?'

'It depends on the question.'

'But a witness has got to answer if you order her to, hasn't she?'

'Yes, if I order her to.'

'And, if she refuses, surely you can tell the jury to disregard her evidence. "Members of the jury," you'll say, "how can you rely on the word of a witness who refuses to answer a perfectly simple question?" – but you can do that sort of thing much better than I can, chum, and you're going to, aren't you?'

'What is the question?'

'You ask her if she's ever been employed by this man.'

He tore a bit of blotting paper off the pad on the judge's desk and wrote a name in pencil on it. He handed it to the judge.

'She'll refuse to answer, and the rest is up to you, chum. Don't look so glum. To win a battle, a soldier has got to have two things. The will to win and the tools to finish the job. You've got the first and I've given you the second. The ball's in your court, chum. And for your own sake see that your shot is a winner. May I go now, please?'

CHAPTER ELEVEN

Problem

The judge sat thinking for a long time after George Ledbury had left. He had from Friday till Monday in which to make up his mind. In spite of what he'd said to George Ledbury, he knew that, if he chose, one way or another he could see to it that the prisoner was acquitted. What *was* his duty? On the face of it, of course, he had to comply with his oath, and he would certainly be breaking it if he did what he had been asked to do. Breaking it through fear. Fear of the consequences. That was exactly what he'd sworn not to do. He had sworn to try cases uninfluenced by the thought of what might happen to him as a result of his conduct of the case. To break that oath would have seemed impossible the day before. And yet the man was right. He had a duty towards Angela. Which was the greater duty – to ensure that a man was properly tried or to save a life? As a lawyer he could see only one answer to the problem: to comply with his oath. But for a layman and a father the answer was far from clear. One had a duty to save lives. Even sometimes at the expense of other lives. Here no other life would be in jeopardy.

He tried to look at the problem as logically as possible. Suppose he himself had been threatened, beyond taking all normal precautions he would disregard such threats.

That was beyond question. Judges are very rarely threatened, and no attempt has been made in modern times to carry out any such threat. Not very long ago a judge's wife was threatened but no attempt was made to follow it up. And the threat was more in the nature of revenge than an attempt to interfere with the judge's conduct of a case. But, whatever had happened in the past, no judge would yield to threats of violence to himself. That was simple. But what about threats of violence to other people? The answer would be the same if the people could be reasonably protected. But suppose the person threatened had, as in this case, been already kidnapped? Suppose it were the Prime Minister or some distinguished man? Did it make any difference who the person was? A life is a life. Is not one life more important than the proper trial of one case? But, if the threat succeeded in the present case, might it not be used in others? Thousands of children play in the streets. All a desperate and determined criminal's desperate and determined friends need do is to kidnap a child, any child, and announce that, unless Bill Bloggins were set free, the child would be murdered. Think of the agony of the innocent parents in such a case. Yet could the community afford to be held up to ransom in this way? Suppose it had been in the days of the death penalty. Unless Bill Bloggins is reprieved and released and allowed to go abroad, Elsie Smith, an innocent child of innocent parents, will be murdered. Would the Home Secretary say: 'I'm sorry, Mr and Mrs Smith, the law must take its course and your child must die.' It would certainly be a very, very unhappy Home Secretary who could do this. But could he afford not to do it? It would mean that the rule of law had gone and that the rule of force had taken its place.

Now he was in the position of such a Home Secretary. Unless he did what he was told, Angela would be murdered. He had no doubt that the man meant what he said. Angela would be murdered. He could not bear it. Why should she and he be compelled to carry such an insufferable burden for the benefit of the state? He had discharged his duties as a judge for many years honourably and reasonably well. Was he now in honour bound to sacrifice his daughter? He would not have spared his own life. After all, he had faced death often enough in war. But this was infinitely worse than any danger to himself. It was intolerable.

Why did he hesitate to comply with George Ledbury's demands? 'You can resign,' he had been told. Of course he could and would. It was not the disgrace – if indeed there were any – which he feared. It was the inviolable tradition of English judges which made him hesitate. And the knowledge that, if he gave in, there might be further victims. If he made a stand, the underworld would know that the scheme wouldn't work. He would be acclaimed on all sides as a hero. And Angela would be dead. He sent for his clerk.

'John,' he said, 'I'm going now. Don't forget, please, not a word to anyone.'

'You look dreadful,' said the clerk. 'Are you ill or what is it?'

'Don't ask questions, please,' said the judge. 'Just do as I ask.'

He left the Old Bailey and started to walk towards his home, still thinking.

CHAPTER TWELVE

Superintendent in the Box

On the following Monday the trial was resumed, but, before Margaret went back into the witness box, Ledbury said that he had a complaint to make.

'What is it?' asked the judge.

'Superintendent Pittville refused to allow me to see my brother.'

'Your brother?' asked the judge. 'When?'

'On Friday afternoon.'

'Mr Stokes,' said the judge, 'will you ask the superintendent to come into the witness box, please.'

'Very good, my lord. Fetch Superintendent Pittville, please, usher.'

'He's the officer in charge of the case?' asked the judge.

'Yes, my lord.'

'Why is he not in Court?'

'He's a witness of fact, my lord.'

'Of course.'

The superintendent came into Court, went into the witness box and was sworn.

'Superintendent,' said the judge, 'the accused complains that you would not allow him to see his brother on Friday. Is that correct?'

'Not entirely, my lord.'

'What happened?'

'A man who said he was the brother of the accused came here and asked if he could see him. I agreed, provided he would allow himself to be searched before and after the visit. He refused. So I said he could apply to see him at Brixton prison. It would then be a matter for the Governor. He said he wanted to see him here. I repeated the conditions. He again refused and the interview ended.'

'Why were such conditions necessary?' asked the judge. 'An officer could have been present during the interview.'

'I'd rather not answer that question in the presence of the jury, my lord.'

'Very well,' said the judge. 'Members of the jury, will you kindly go outside the court for a few minutes. Please don't leave the corridor.'

'Well, superintendent?' said the judge when the jury box was empty.

'This is no ordinary case, my lord. From information in my possession I am satisfied there is no length to which the accused and his associates would not go to free him.'

'But, if an officer were present, he could see that nothing was handed over.'

'My lord, this is a little embarrassing to say, and I want to make it plain that I am personally sure that all the officers here are fully trustworthy. But there is the very occasional man in the Force who is not proof against temptation. Some escapes from prisons have proved this. A couple of hundred pounds – or even more – is a lot to a man earning a police officer's pay. Even a superintendent's, my lord.'

'But why couldn't you be present, superintendent?'

'For the same reason, my lord. If the accused subsequently escaped, I shouldn't want it to be suggested that it could have been my fault. These people will stop at nothing, my lord. Violence, bribery, it's all the same to them. Your lordship may think I'm exaggerating, but I'm not, my lord. So the only sure way to be certain one brother didn't help the other to escape was by not letting them see each other without the visiting brother being searched. If the governor of the prison allows the interview, that's his responsibility.'

'You hear what the officer says, Mr Ledbury,' said the judge. 'Do you want to say anything more or ask any questions?'

'Just one question,' said Ledbury. 'When I saw my brother at Brixton he told me – '

'You saw him at Brixton? Then what on earth are you complaining about?' said the judge.

'My brother is a very busy man. It was very inconvenient for him to go to Brixton.'

'Don't let's waste any more time. Let the jury return at once,' said the judge.

'I hope your lordship isn't going to run the case against me just because you think I made a frivolous complaint,' said Ledbury. 'A little while ago you offered me a new trial before a fresh judge and jury. I think I'd like to accept your offer now.'

'It's too late.'

'Oh – well – I shall have to make do with what there is.'

'Behave yourself.'

'Suppose I don't?'

'I warned you on Friday of the consequences.'

'I know you did. I just wondered if they'd be the same today.'

'They would be the same today,' said the judge. 'Let the jury return.'

'My lord,' said Stokes, a few minutes later, 'as the superintendent is in the witness box, I wondered if his evidence could be heard straightaway. It's rather inconvenient having him out of court, and his evidence is quite short. Unless, of course, the accused objects.'

'Do you object, Mr Ledbury?'

'I don't mind in the least. He's not likely to tell the truth any more this afternoon than he is this morning.'

'Very well,' said the judge, 'let the superintendent give his evidence.'

'Superintendent,' said Stokes, 'you were the officer in charge of the enquiries in this case and did you in consequence pay a visit to the accused at his home in South Kensington?'

'I did.'

'When did you see the accused?'

'At about 11 am on the 23rd August.'

'What took place between you?'

'After I'd satisfied myself as to his identity I told the accused that I was making enquiries about a number of cases of blackmail and that I thought he could give me some information about them.'

'What did he say?'

'He said that he didn't know what I was talking about.'

'And what did you say?'

'I asked him if he'd mind answering some questions and he said he would mind. I said that that was strange if he was a completely innocent man. He said there was nothing strange about it. He didn't like the police or their methods. I said that if he wouldn't answer questions in his home I'd take him to the police station.'

'You had no right to do that,' said the judge.

'No, my lord.'

'Then why did you do it?'

'If we didn't do it, we couldn't collect half the criminals we do.'

'That may be. Have you never heard of the Judges' Rules?'

'Only too well, my lord. I'm sorry, my lord. I shouldn't have said that.'

'No. Those rules are framed to protect accused people.'

'I know, my lord, but the police have a very difficult and often dangerous job to do, and we're hamstrung at every turn.'

'Behave yourself, superintendent. Continue with your evidence.'

'Well, what happened, superintendent?' asked Stokes.

'The accused refused to come to the police station.'

'Did you take him there?'

'No, my lord.'

'So what you said was pure bluff?' said the judge.

'Not entirely, my lord. When I said it, I intended to take him, but, when I found that he knew I'd no right to do so, I changed my mind.'

'Well, what happened?'

'I said I was going to question him whether he liked it or not. I had a duty to do and I was going to discharge it.'

'What did he say?'

'He told me to go.'

'What did you do?'

'I stayed. I sat down in a chair. He told me to get up.'

'What did you do?'

'I remained seated.'

'This is all very interesting,' said the judge, 'but how does it help the jury?'

'The conversation did continue, my lord,' said Stokes.

'Well, what was said, superintendent?'

'I mentioned a number of names to the accused and asked if he had heard of them. He said he might have done so. One of the names I mentioned was Hugh Bridges. He said he'd read about the case.'

'I object to this evidence, my lord,' said Ledbury.

'On what ground?'

'I hadn't been cautioned.'

'Is that true, superintendent?'

'Yes, my lord.'

'Had you made up your mind to charge the accused when you were questioning him?'

'Well, my lord, the position was this – '

'Would you answer the question, please. Had you made up your mind to charge him?'

'Well, my lord, the position was this – '

'You have said that before – will you kindly answer the question.'

'My lord,' said Stokes, 'I do respectfully suggest that the superintendent should be allowed to answer in his own way.'

'This was a perfectly simple question to which the answer could have been yes or no.'

'My lord, might I say – ' began the superintendent.

'Be quiet,' said the judge.

'My lord – I must very respectfully ask you not to – not to bully the superintendent,' said Stokes.

'I beg your pardon?!' said the judge.

'If I put it too strongly, I apologise, my lord,' said Stokes, who felt he had gone too far in the superintendent's defence.

But the judge was apparently also not happy about his own behaviour. 'I'm sorry, superintendent,' he said. 'I didn't intend – '

'Thank you, my lord.'

'Now perhaps you'd answer the question – in your own way,' said the judge.

'I personally felt satisfied on evidence in my possession that the accused was behind all these blackmail cases and I hoped to be able to arrest him but I wanted to see what he said first.'

'Suppose he had refused to answer any questions, would you have arrested him?'

'I think so, my lord, but I'd have had to consider the matter.'

'Then surely he should have been cautioned, Mr Stokes.'

'It's a border-line case, my lord,' said Stokes, 'and in my submission it's within your lordship's discretion to admit the evidence.'

'Or to refuse to. I ask you to refuse,' said Ledbury.

'I ask you to admit it,' said Stokes.

'If I admit it, is it likely to provide further evidence against the accused corroborating Miss Vane?'

'Certainly, my lord, or I would not tender it.'

'Apart from her evidence you haven't really any direct evidence against the accused?'

'That is so, my lord.'

'So that, apart from this additional evidence, if for some reason she breaks down and her evidence can't be relied upon, the accused must be acquitted.'

'I think I must agree to that, my lord.'

'So my decision on this matter might be of vital importance?'

'Indeed so, my lord.'

'Do you wish to say any more about it, Mr Stokes?'

'No, thank you, my lord.'

'Mr Ledbury?'

'Yes, my lord. The papers have been full of this case for weeks. My name's been bandied about all over the place.

Everyone thinks I'm guilty. That's just because they want to pin the blame on someone. If I'm acquitted, they'll have got nothing for their money. They'll feel cheated. I ask you not to do the same, my lord. You're a judge and you hold the scales of justice. Don't tilt them against me. If they should be tilted at all, they should be tilted in my favour. That's the law of England. Better a hundred guilty men acquitted than one innocent man convicted.'

'That may be what a lot of people think,' said the judge, 'and it may be right but it is not the law of England. The law simply says that no one shall be convicted of a crime unless the case is proved against him. No more, no less.'

'But surely, if there's a doubt,' said Ledbury, 'it should be resolved in favour of an accused person.'

'If there's a doubt, the case is not proved.'

'But if you've a doubt whether to let in evidence or not, surely you should resolve it in my favour.'

'There is something in that,' conceded the judge.

'Well – you must have a doubt or you wouldn't have taken so long to give a decision on the matter.'

'Some judges take hours to give a decision but they've never had any real doubt about it.'

'Not you, my lord, I'm sure.'

'Is that all you have to say?'

'Yes, my lord.'

The judge considered for a short time. Then: 'I shall admit the evidence,' he said.

'Is that a wise decision, my lord?' said Ledbury.

'Don't be impertinent. If you disagree with it and are convicted you can appeal.'

'It might be too late then.'

'What exactly do you mean by that?'

'What do I mean?' said Ledbury. 'Oh, nothing.'

'Go on, please, Mr Stokes,' said the judge.

'Well, superintendent, will you please continue. You mentioned Hugh Bridges.'

'The accused said he'd read about him and that he was a poor fish anyway.'

'Did he say anything else?'

'Yes, my lord. He said it was an odd coincidence but he'd once known a boy at Bridges' school, St Augusta's.'

'Did he mention it by name?'

'Yes.'

'What did you say?'

'I asked him to repeat it. He did so and I wrote it down.'

'And then what?'

'I said to the accused – how are you able to say you knew someone at St Augusta's when the name of Mr Bridges' school was never mentioned in the Press?'

'What did he say?'

'He looked a bit taken aback and then said he was sure it was. I told him it wasn't. He paused for some time and then said: "Well, if it wasn't in the newspapers, someone must have told me." '

'Go on,' said Stokes.

'I said: "Who told you?" He said: "How can I tell? You know how things get around in blackmail cases. They call a man Mr B but dozens of people know who he is and talk about it." "So that gives your people a firmer hold of them," I put in. "I resent that," he said.'

'How did the conversation end?'

'The accused said he must have picked up the name of the school by way of gossip.'

'How did he know the name of Bridges if he was called Mr B?' asked the judge.

'He wasn't called Mr B. Mr Bridges preferred to give evidence under his own name.'

'Later,' continued Stokes, 'you arrested the accused, cautioned and charged him?'

'Yes.'

'What did he say?'

'He said, "I'd like to know who's behind this." I said that he'd know that in due course. He said: "Well, whoever it is, he's barking up the wrong tree. I've never been a party to blackmailing anyone in my life." '

'Thank you, superintendent,' said Stokes and sat down.

'Yes, Mr Ledbury?' said the judge, inviting him to cross-examine.

'Superintendent,' began Ledbury, 'you'd do anything to get me convicted, wouldn't you?'

'Certainly not.'

'Well – you'd take a lot of trouble?'

'I take a lot of trouble over all my cases.'

'When you came to see me – you'd only got the evidence of the girl, hadn't you?'

'Substantially, yes. We had statements from Jones and Nottingham but substantially no *evidence* against you except Miss Vane's.'

'So, if you could get a bit more at the interview, that would be all to the good.'

'It was my duty to get evidence by any proper means.'

'Including carting me off to the police station?'

'I didn't take you to the police station.'

'But you threatened to.'

'I've already said so.'

'Superintendent, you've had a lot of experience in getting evidence in criminal cases?'

'Of course.'

'Isn't it a very old trick to say that a suspected person has mentioned something which he couldn't have known unless he'd been concerned in the crime? A man is charged, say, with murdering a woman – none of the papers have said how she was killed and the accused, when questioned, says: "I never strangled her." How did he know she was strangled?'

'Yes, that happens.'

'But, of course, if a police officer has very conveniently told the accused that the woman was strangled, his answer would be quite normal. That happens, doesn't it?'

'I have not known it to happen.'

'But it could happen?'

'Anything *can* happen.'

'I suggest to you that you yourself tried it on me in this case.'

'What are you suggesting?' asked the judge.

'I'm suggesting to the superintendent that he told me the name of the school and that it was after that I said it was odd but I'd known a boy from that school.'

'Did you mention the name of the school, superintendent?' asked the judge.

'Certainly not, my lord.'

'Never?' asked Ledbury.

'Never.'

'But,' said Ledbury, 'you've admitted that you said to me: "How are you able to say the school was St Augusta's?" '

'That was after you'd mentioned the name.'

'But you've just sworn you *never* mentioned it to me.'

'I meant before you did.'

'You didn't say that. You said "Never".'

'That was a slip.'

'Any other slips in your evidence, superintendent?'

'None that I know of.'

'Who mentioned the name of the school first?' asked the judge.

'He did, my lord.'

'Are you sure?'

'Absolutely, my lord.'

'Well – of course, he says that now, my lord,' said Ledbury, 'now he's got the point.'

'Have you any further questions to ask?'

'It doesn't seem much use. Everyone's against me. I don't suppose I shall ever see my family again – my wife – or little daughter. If you send me away for forty years – she's as good as dead to me.'

CHAPTER THIRTEEN

Margaret's Cross-examination Continued

After a short pause the judge said: 'Mr Ledbury – you're an educated and intelligent man. You know perfectly well that this case is not over, that you are presumed to be innocent until you are found guilty and that you have not been found guilty. So kindly stop talking nonsense, and let us get on with the trial.'

'Very well, my lord,' said Ledbury, 'but it's not nonsense.'

And there was some menace in his voice as he said it.

'Thank you, superintendent. Miss Vane, will you go back to the witness box, please.'

'Tell me, Miss Vane,' said Ledbury, 'how much money have you received altogether for your part in this affair?'

'A newspaper has paid me a fee of £5,000.'

'That's a lot of money.'

'I was risking my life and still am.'

'Suppose I'm convicted, will you get any more?'

'If I live to enjoy it I expect I shall.'

'Do you not *know*?'

'I don't know for certain but I was originally offered a fee of £5,000 with a promise of more if my investigations were successful.'

'If I were sent to prison for forty or fifty years, presumably you'd call that a success?'

'Five or ten would do.'

'So you want me to be convicted?'

'With all my heart and soul.'

'There's nothing you'd like more?'

'Oh yes, there is – I'd like to see your brother convicted too.'

'Oh, come, we weren't both in the park with you.'

'No, but I've no doubt you're in it together – and he's behind the attempts to prevent my giving evidence.'

'Have you any proof of that?'

'Unfortunately not.'

'But you'd do anything to secure my conviction?'

'I'd do anything lawful.'

'But you've done unlawful things too, like smuggling.'

'That's true.'

'And blackmail?'

'On the face of it, yes.'

'Then how are the jury to know where you'd draw the line? A little matter of perjury, for example? Wouldn't you tell a lie to get me convicted?'

'No.'

'Why not?'

'Because I wouldn't.'

'Wouldn't you? If you'd risk other people's lives in order to get me, surely you'd risk a bit for yourself.'

'I'm in considerable personal danger as it is and you know it.'

'Let's assume you are. And all this is because you've set out to get me in the dock?'

'Well?'

'Well – having risked so much why wouldn't you risk a bit more and tell a lie to get the jury to convict me?'

'It isn't necessary to lie. I've told the truth and I hope you'll be convicted on that.'

'But, if you felt that I might be slipping out of your clutches, would you scruple to tell a lie if it served your purpose better than the truth?'

'I've sworn to tell the truth.'

'Does the oath make any difference to you?'

'Of course it does.'

'Do you mean that?'

'Certainly.'

'I suggest to you that it makes no difference to you at all.'

'You can suggest what you like but it does.'

'Let us see. Tell me, would you tell lies to the police to harm me?'

'No.'

'Quite sure?'

'Certainly.'

'What you said in court on Friday was roughly what you told the police?'

'It was part of what I told the police.'

'And you say what you told the police was true?'

'Yes.'

'Then will you kindly tell me what difference the oath made to you?'

'How d'you mean?'

'You said it made a difference, but if you equally told the truth whether you were on oath or not, it made no difference at all, did it?'

'I see what you mean.'

'Well – did the oath make any difference?'

'If you put it like that, I suppose not.'

'But you swore that it did. Three times.'

'What d'you expect me to say to that?'

'I expect you to tell the truth this time and say that the oath made no difference.'

'Well – I suppose it didn't.'

'Then why did you swear it did?'

'I don't really know.'

'Don't you? It was because you felt you ought to say that the oath made a difference.'

'Perhaps so.'

'Yet three times you gave me the same answer – on oath.'

'You've made your point, Mr Ledbury,' said the judge. 'Will you go on to the next one, please.'

'May I not conduct my case in my own way, my lord? The result of this trial is very important for me.'

'It's very important for everyone.'

'I should have said everyone,' said Ledbury and looked straight at the judge.

'What is your next question?'

'I want a little time to think,' said Ledbury.

CHAPTER FOURTEEN

Conversation Between Brothers

Ledbury was thinking of the conversation he had had with his brother George in Brixton. They had been allowed an interview in private, in view of the fact that Ledbury was defending himself.

'I think it's all right,' George had said. 'The old boy is scared stiff. He dotes on his little girl. He's not giving up without a struggle but, when it comes to the pinch, he'll give in. After all, it's human nature.'

'But these bloody judges,' he had said, 'aren't human. They're bits of parchment. At any rate in court they are. I dare say some of them have fun and games outside court, but, when they're in a court, they're like clockwork. They're books, not men.'

'Well, this one is a man all right,' George had said. 'You should have seen him. I put him through his paces like a trainer with a performing bear.'

'I've no doubt you had a high old time, George, but that's not much use to me if he won't play ball.'

'He'll play ball all right.'

'D'you think I'd better give him an occasional reminder?'

'Not half a bad idea. Bring in something about *your* little daughter. You haven't got one but he's not to know.'

'Right, I will. Something about not seeing her again if I go to prison for forty years?'

'Fine. But not too often. One of the things we've got to look out for is someone spotting that the trial's all phoney. Then the Attorney-General or someone might come and intervene. I told him that. "You've got to act for your life," I said. "Or rather for your little girl's. It's got to appear genuine all through."'

'He's too bloody genuine for my liking at the moment.'

'Well, of course he is. And even now, no one ought to be able to notice a change except you. We don't care if there's no change to notice, so long as he gets the jury to say "not guilty".'

'Suppose they don't? Can you spring me as we leave the court?'

'That's hopeless. They've got pretty well an army there. And armed. There'd be a bloody great battle and nothing to show for it but a few dead bodies. Yours one of them perhaps. No, if this doesn't work, we'll have to wait a bit.'

'I hope to God it does. I don't feel like waiting a bit. I've never been inside before. If it's like this on remand, God knows what it's like when you're convicted.'

'You aren't going to be convicted, Cliff. I've fixed it. It wasn't a dream, you know. I really saw the old man himself, and told him what'll happen if he doesn't play. And he knows I mean it.'

'How often d'you think I should give him a reminder?' he had asked.

'Not too often. Two or three times. Not more. Too suspicious. But you wait. He'll have to bide his time. But, when the right moment comes, he'll pop the question and it'll be over. Now cheer up. We'll meet in Mexico City on Tuesday. I'll have to go straightaway. They'll be after me as soon as you're let out. Your seat's booked. Everything's ready.'

'Well, let's hope you're right. It's easy to be optimistic in your position. You can be in Mexico when you like. I can only be there if the jury likes.'

'They'll like, old boy. I wouldn't leave you here if I wasn't as sure as I could be that it'll work. If you had a little girl, you'd say or do anything to save her. So would I. And so would anyone, a judge or anyone else. And he'll have the whole weekend to think about it. He won't be sitting on the Bench on Saturday or Sunday. But at his home. Where his daughter ought to be but isn't. Wondering, waiting. Forty-eight hours of that will reduce him to pulp. He'll eat out of your hand. But, if he's wise, he won't show it. Not too obviously, anyway.'

CHAPTER FIFTEEN

To Ask or Not to Ask

While Ledbury was thinking of his conversation with his brother, the judge was apparently thinking too. Suddenly he said: 'Miss Vane, while the accused is thinking of his next question, I wonder if you'd answer one of mine.'

'Certainly, my lord,' said Margaret.

This is it, thought Ledbury. Good old George. Here it comes. At that moment Stokes, who had been in conversation with the Director of Public Prosecutions and had not heard what the judge had said, rose and intervened.

'My lord,' he said, 'I wondered if this would be a convenient moment for me – '

This was too much for Ledbury.

'Mr Stokes,' he said, 'didn't you hear? His lordship wants to ask a question.'

'Thank you, Mr Ledbury,' said the judge, 'I'm quite capable of looking after myself. Yes, what is it, Mr Stokes?'

'But the question you wanted to ask, my lord,' Ledbury could not restrain himself from saying.

'I've decided not to ask it.'

Blast Stokes, thought Ledbury. He's ruined it all. The old man has taken the interruption as a sign from Heaven that he shouldn't ask the question. Blast and curse!

'Not for the moment, at any rate,' continued the judge.

Thank God for that, thought Ledbury. There's still a chance. I must bring him back to it.

'Yes, what is it, Mr Stokes?' said the judge.

'My lord, I wanted to refer to my application to call fresh evidence.'

'You've served notice on the prisoner?'

'Yes, my lord.'

'Well, I'll deal with that when this witness' evidence has finished.'

'Very good, my lord,' said Stokes and sat down.

'Go on, Mr Ledbury, please,' said the judge.

I must give him a jerk, thought Ledbury. Let me think. Where shall I begin? I know. He wrote the name 'Slaughter' on a piece of paper.

'Miss Vane, you know this name, don't you?'

He handed the paper to the usher who took it to Margaret. She looked at it.

'Yes, I do.'

'Did you pretend to him that you came from a thing called the Institute for Cleaner Morals and blackmail him to the tune of hundreds of pounds.'

'On the face of it, I did.'

'On the face of it! You threatened him with exposure if he didn't pay, didn't you?'

'Yes.'

'And he paid to avoid exposure to his wife and his parish. He was a keen churchgoer, wasn't he? I don't want to make a mistake about this man.'

'No, that's the one.'

'Well, where does "on the face of it" come in? You made the threats, he paid because of them and you had the money.'

'I passed it on to Nottingham.'

'You kept some for yourself.'

'That's true but I handed it over to Mr X and the man whose name you've written down got back the whole amount he'd paid eventually.'

'From whom?'

'From one of the newspapers for whom Mr X wrote.'

'What was this Institute for Cleaner Morals?'

'You were.'

'That's an absolute lie. I have never had a penny of the money. There isn't a scrap of evidence that I had anything to do with it.'

'You admitted it to me.'

'In our so-called walk in the park, d'you mean?'

'Yes.'

'Let me ask you about this walk. Had you been to the police before it?'

'No.'

'Why not?'

'Mr X thought we ought to get the evidence first and then go to the police.'

'Did Mr X know me by sight?'

'Yes, he did.'

'Exactly. I suggest to you that you invented this interview, and picked me out because Mr X pointed me out to you at some stage.'

'Rubbish.'

'Don't talk like that, please, Miss Vane,' said the judge.

'I'm sorry, my lord.'

'But is it such rubbish?' went on the judge. 'Mr X knew the accused by sight?'

'Yes, but it wasn't he who pointed out the accused to me. It was Jones.'

'We've only your word for it,' said Ledbury. 'I suggest to you that you were the brains behind this blackmail racket and, when the pace got too hot, you had to put the blame on someone, so you tried me.'

'Why on earth should I try to fix the blame on you – if you were completely innocent?'

'Yes – why should she?' asked the judge.

Now's my chance, thought Ledbury.

'Are you leading for the prosecution, my lord,' he said, 'or sitting impartially to do what's right – without fear or favour, affection or ill will – that's how it goes, isn't it?'

'Mr Ledbury, I regret that I must take the unusual course of dealing with you here and now for contempt of court. I fine you £100,' said the judge.

'That's a foolish thing to do, my lord.'

'I fine you a further £200.'

'It's going to prove an expensive case for someone, my lord, very expensive.'

Ledbury's eyes met the judge's. They looked at each other for a second or two and then Ledbury looked away. Am I going too far? he thought.

'I'm sorry, my lord,' he said. 'I'm rather on edge.'

'Very well,' said the judge. 'I'll rise for a few minutes for you to recover yourself.'

CHAPTER SIXTEEN

The Question

The judge rose and left the court. Ledbury was taken down to the cells. He was not altogether happy. The fine he did not mind in the least. In one way it was a good thing. The judge had been told to make things look genuine and he was quite right to fine him. But was he acting or did he mean it? It was impossible to tell. If George were right, that was as it should be. But suppose he were wrong? It didn't bear thinking about. He had had a most enjoyable life up till then. Most of the good things had come his way. If they hadn't come, he'd taken them. And now to be kept in prison for years. Clifton Ledbury was a good advertisement for original sin. He had been bad from the start. He had had every chance. A happy home. One mother and one father. A normal education. Sufficient money to get started. Everything in fact which should help to keep a person in the civilised ranks of society. But in his mind he had never conformed. He had none of the virtues, though, of course, he could appear to have them when necessary. He did not love his fellow men and women. Obviously there had been women whom he had loved physically and men whom he liked. And he was fond of his brother George. There was indeed a strange bond between the two brothers. Perhaps this was because

George was also bad. So long as they got what they themselves wanted they did not in the least care what happened to anyone else. Wickedness is normally due to environment or heredity or a mixture of both. In the case of the Ledbury brothers, as far as could be traced, it was due to neither. Each brother was born with the spark of sin in him and, as they grew up, the spark became an unquenchable fire.

As Ledbury sat in the cells wondering what was going on in the judge's mind, he would have prayed, if he had known how. But he had no one to pray to. So he could only wish. And he had never wished so hard. He was trying to reach the judge with his waves of wishes. He actually wondered if telepathy could go as far as this. Could the mind of the prisoner sitting on a wooden chair in his cell reach the mind of the judge sitting on a comfortable chair in his room? In fact the judge was not sitting. He was walking up and down. But that should have made no difference in principle.

The judge's clerk was with him as he paced up and down. 'You've told me not to ask any questions,' he said, 'and I won't. But do me a favour, sir. When this case is over, take a bit of a holiday. If it's only a week – or a weekend.'

'Yes,' said the judge, 'when the case is over, I'll take Angela away for the weekend.'

'Good,' said the clerk and then added almost casually, 'Is she enjoying herself sir?'

'She's all right,' said the judge gruffly, 'she's all right.'

'I forget where you said she was, sir. By the sea, was it?'

The judge affected not to have heard.

'I must get back to court in a moment.'

'Will you finish today?'

'I certainly hope so. I'll sit a bit late, if necessary.'

Meanwhile the superintendent and Stokes were talking.

'I hope the judge is all right,' said Stokes. 'He doesn't seem at all well to me.'

'I believe he has some illness at home,' said the superintendent. 'I expect that's worrying him.'

'But he's behaving so oddly,' said Stokes. 'Look at the way he dealt with your evidence. Usually he makes up his mind and sticks to it. But this time he wavered to and fro and then, when I thought he was going to down us, he let the evidence in. Very strange.'

'Of course, sir, some judges are like that.'

'I know,' said Stokes, 'but not Hereford. He's a strong judge. Even when he's wrong, he's quite sure about it. There are no half measures with him. And the way he treats Ledbury is so odd. At one moment he lets him cheek him and doesn't move a muscle. Then suddenly he clamps down on him and fines him.'

'Yes, I noticed that,' said the superintendent. 'But I suppose he doesn't want to alienate the jury. Judges always give a lot of rope to prisoners when they're defending themselves, don't they, sir?'

'That's true,' said Stokes.

'Let's hope he hangs himself with it,' said the superintendent. 'If ever I wanted to down a villain, I want to now. I'll be really angry if he gets away. D'you think he's a chance, sir?'

'If the jury believes the girl, he's had it.'

'D'you think they will, sir?'

'Your guess is as good as mine. But, if I had to bet, I'd put my money on her. Her evidence sounds true. The little mistakes she makes are those of an honest witness, not a liar. And I don't think he'll get anywhere with her apparent blackmailing activities. It was the only way to find him. She's done a wonderful job.'

'I'm with you there, sir. Wonderful. How right I was to let her go when we picked her up. It was taking a chance, I grant you. But I believed her. One of my inspectors thought I'd fallen for her.'

'I shouldn't have blamed you. She's a fine-looking girl.'

'Really, sir! It should take more than a fine-looking girl to bowl me over.'

'Sorry, superintendent,' said Stokes, 'I wasn't serious. But I am serious when I say that *I* think she's quite an exceptional person. Think of the courage it required. And the intelligence. I think we're all right, superintendent. Of course, he's clever too. But he's got to deny this interview ever took place. Why should she make it up? And if the interview did take place, that's the end of the case. It would have been more sensible of him to admit that he met the girl but to deny the conversation.'

'I suppose his difficulty there, sir, is to explain why she met him. There's no doubt it can be proved that she was getting money out of people. It's equally clear that she was doing it on instructions. Why should she meet him? What for?'

'Will he admit to knowing Nottingham and Jones or not, d'you think?' asked Stokes.

'There's no reason why he should. He'll never be confronted with them. Nor will anyone else in my view. That girl wouldn't have been available, if she hadn't been very lucky.'

Ledbury had been right in thinking that Margaret wanted to see him convicted. Above all things. Above all things but one, that is. She wanted her lover nursed back to life above all things. But next to that she wanted Ledbury behind bars. A desire for revenge is not a pretty quality but there is no doubt that Margaret had it in full. Not because she had nearly been killed herself. She was a girl who liked excitement and who had had plenty of it in her life. But Ledbury had been responsible for gravely injuring the one person in the world whom she adored, and she would gladly have killed him herself. She was quite capable of doing so. And she had even considered ways and means of disposing of him, if he were acquitted. She was a highly emotional girl. Her parents, like Ledbury's, had been normal respectable people. But they had neither her intelligence nor courage. She had been at school until she was eighteen and then she had rushed into life seeking excitement. For five years she had tried the stage but this did not satisfy her needs. She needed something far more frightening. She was the ideal person to undertake the job for which she had been engaged. Because, though she was emotional, she had no difficulty in subduing her emotions when she had a job in hand. Thus she could calmly undertake the task of blackmailing people without allowing the natural pity which she had for some of the victims to affect her actions.

It was ten minutes before the judge returned to court. Ledbury thought that he would try one further probe. The judge bowed first to counsel, then to the jury, and then sat down.

'Aren't I in the case too?' asked Ledbury. 'Is there any reason why you don't bow to me too?'

Everyone waited for an explosion. It is quite true that today many judges will treat an unconvicted prisoner with proper courtesy, though there are still a few who insist on calling him by his surname without the prefix of 'Mr', whereas they treat other witnesses with ordinary politeness. But the idea of bowing to the prisoner does not yet seem to have occurred to anyone. Nevertheless the prisoner is very much a part of a case and there seems no logical reason why he should not be treated by the judge in the same way as the jury and counsel are treated, except, of course, that, if he is not on bail, he is locked up at night and they are not. But the sheer impertinence of the request made a big impact on those present and you could almost hear an intake of breath. There was a pause. Then the judge rose, bowed to Ledbury and said: 'You're quite right. I'm sorry.'

'Thank you, my lord,' said Ledbury and felt very much reassured. But I hope he doesn't overdo it, he said to himself.

Just after Margaret had gone back into the witness box Ledbury suddenly said: 'What's that juryman doing?'

'What on earth d'you mean?' said the judge.

'He passed a note to the next one,' said Ledbury.

'Why shouldn't he?'

'How do we know it's about the case? It might be about the 2.30.'

'Mr Foreman,' said the judge, 'was a note passed round the jury?'

'Yes, my lord.'

'Was it about the case?'

'Certainly, my lord.'

'Perhaps they want to stop the case, my lord,' said Ledbury.

'Well, they can't till the case for the prosecution is closed.'

'This is the last witness.'

'But you haven't finished your cross-examination.'

'If the jury want to stop the case, I'll sit down right now.'

'Do you want to stop the case, Mr Foreman?' asked the judge.

'Really, my lord,' said Stokes, 'with the greatest possible respect, I do object to your lordship asking that question at this stage. Not only is the witness still being cross-examined but I have the right to re-examine.'

'Do you wish to do so?'

'With the greatest respect, my lord, I'm not bound to answer that question.'

'Why shouldn't you?' said Ledbury.

'Mr Stokes, is there any objection to *my* asking you that question?' said the judge. 'Yes, what is it, Mr Foreman?' For at that moment the man on the extreme right of the front row of the jury box had stood up.

'If it would be of any help to you, my lord,' he said, 'the jury has no intention whatever of stopping the case at this stage. It seems to the jury that there is a strong case for the accused to answer.'

He sat down and there was silence for several seconds.

'I see,' said the judge.

'It's the way you're running the case against me,' said Ledbury. 'There's no justice in this country for the man in the dock.'

'I sincerely hope there is – for you and everyone else.'

'Three cheers,' said Ledbury.

'I shall fine you a further five hundred pounds.'

'Will you take a cheque?'

'You can have seven days to pay – one thousand pounds. Now please continue your cross-examination.'

'I've forgotten where I was.'

'Take your time.'

'Thank you. Perhaps you'd like to ask a question while I'm thinking?'

'Miss Vane, there *is* a question I'd like to ask you,' said the judge. 'I'd like to know if you were ever employed by this man? Hand this to the witness, please, usher.'

The judge handed a piece of paper to the usher who took it to Margaret.

Thank God! thought Ledbury. I was taking the hell of a chance but it came off.

'Well?' said the judge.

Margaret said nothing.

'Miss Vane,' repeated the judge, 'were you ever employed by this man?'

'My lord,' replied Margaret eventually after a further pause, 'I'm sorry – but I'm not prepared to answer any questions whatever on this subject.'

'Why not?'

'My lord, I can only say that I am not prepared to answer any such questions.'

'Might the answers incriminate you? If I were satisfied of that, I could excuse you from answering.'

'I am not prepared to answer, my lord.'

'But you must answer.'

'I'm afraid I can't.'

'Can't or won't?'

'Won't, my lord.'

'Mr Stokes,' said the judge, 'perhaps you would have a word with the witness and point out the seriousness of her position.'

Well done! thought Ledbury. You had to do something like that. It's all going very nicely.

'Certainly, my lord. As a matter of fact, I should like to make application for leave to call an additional witness and, while your lordship is dealing with that matter, someone from the Director's office will have a word with Miss Vane.'

'You can have as many words as you like,' said Margaret. 'I'm not going to answer.'

'Don't be foolish, Miss Vane,' said the judge. 'Now leave the box, please, and go and have a word with the gentleman sitting in front of Mr Stokes.'

Margaret left the witness box and went out of court with one of the Director's assistants.

'Now, Mr Stokes,' said the judge, 'what is your application?'

'To call an additional witness, my lord.'

'I know but it's a very late stage of the case to do that.'

'Yes, my lord, but we only heard of the witness this morning.'

'That may be, but is it fair to the accused to put extra evidence in at this stage?'

That's the stuff, thought Ledbury.

'It is in the interests of justice, my lord,' said Stokes.

'You say you've given the accused a note of the evidence?'

'As best we could, my lord. It's very short for the reason I've mentioned.'

'Does it add to the strength of the case against the accused?'

'It does indeed, my lord.'

'If Miss Vane's evidence were rejected by the jury – would it make a case against the accused?'

'It might, my lord, and it certainly corroborates Miss Vane indirectly.'

'It's very unfortunate you didn't have the evidence before.'

'It is, my lord, but that is no fault of the prosecution. The witness was unknown to us. He read the papers and came in this morning.'

'If he'd come tomorrow it would have been too late.'

'Indeed, my lord. But he came today.'

'Why isn't it too late today?' asked the judge.

'Because, my lord, justice requires that all of the evidence available should be put before the jury.'

'You keep on talking about justice, as though I were unaware of it,' said the judge rather irritably.

'I'm sorry, my lord. I didn't intend to convey that impression.'

'The interests of the accused have to be considered. That's part of justice too.'

'Of course, my lord. But so are the interests of the public. This is a terrible case, my lord, and – '

'Please don't make speeches to the jury, Mr Stokes. Mr Ledbury, what do you say about this application?'

'I ask you to refuse to entertain it, my lord,' said Ledbury. 'The prosecution has all the organisation and opportunities for getting their case ready. Why should they be allowed to pop things in at the last moment? I may not be able to deal with the witness at such short notice.'

'I should always be prepared to consent to an adjournment if it was necessary,' put in Stokes.

'Don't interrupt, Mr Stokes, please,' said the judge. 'The accused didn't interrupt you. Don't interrupt him.'

'I'm sorry, my lord,' said Stokes, surprised at such an attack.

'I should think so.'

'Really, my lord,' said Stokes a little indignantly, 'all I did was to – '

'Be quiet, Mr Stokes.'

'My lord, really – '

'Be quiet. I want to think.'

'Of course, my lord.'

'Don't be impertinent, Mr Stokes.'

'My lord, really I didn't intend – '

'Please BE QUIET,' said the judge emphatically. 'Now, Mr Ledbury, do you wish to say anything else?'

'No, my lord.'

'Mr Stokes?'

'Only that justice requires – '

'You've said that a hundred times.'

'Three, to be accurate, my lord – and it is the main ground of my application – justice.'

After a short pause during which the judge was apparently having an internal struggle, he said: 'I shall admit the evidence. Call the witness.'

CHAPTER SEVENTEEN

William Morgan

William Morgan came slowly in at the court door and slowly made his way to the witness box. He did not actually limp and so gave the impression of deliberately going slowly. He looked about sixty years old.

'Come along, please,' said the judge impatiently, but Morgan did not move any faster.

'Please don't waste time,' said the judge, and, as Morgan reached the witness box, he added: 'Not another sprained ankle, I hope.'

'I'm sorry, my lord,' said Morgan. 'I've only one leg.' The judge was much distressed.

'Oh, forgive me,' he said. 'You walk remarkably well.'

'Too slowly, I'm afraid, my lord.'

'I apologise. Would you prefer to sit down?'

'No, thank you, my lord. It's nothing. I'm quite used to it. I lost it twenty-six years ago.'

'In the war?'

'I was an air-gunner, my lord.'

'Well, I'm glad you manage so well.'

'Thank you, my lord. It's amazing what one can do without, if necessary.'

'Quite so.'

'My wife left me soon after my leg.'

'I'm sorry,' said the judge. Normally he would have told the witness to be quiet but in view of what had gone before he felt he could not reprimand him.

'She ran away with a man with two legs,' went on Morgan, who was obviously enjoying himself. 'However, I found another wife with two legs too – jolly good ones if I may say so.'

'Has the witness been sworn?' said the judge uncomfortably.

'Not yet, my lord,' said Stokes.

'Take the book in your right hand and repeat the words on the card,' said the clerk.

'I'll have to get out my glasses,' said Morgan. 'I can never find the blooming things. I was lucky with my eyes. Nearly went blind. But I had a wonderful fellow – put them both right. I can see as well as anyone now. Forgive me, my lord. I know I've got them with me. Ah – here they are. Bother, these are distance. I did try bifocals, my lord, but I could never get on with them. I see you have a pair, my lord. How do you find them?'

'Mr Morgan, kindly find your glasses and take the oath,' said the judge firmly. He still did not feel that he could be more severe with the witness. He disliked witnesses who enjoyed themselves in the witness box and usually gave them short shrift. But in this one instance he felt he must control himself. The man had lost a leg in the service of his country and he had reproved him for it. He could only make up for it by giving him a latitude which he would not have shown to anyone else.

'Ah – here they really are,' said Morgan. 'I swear by Almighty God that the evidence I shall give to the court shall be the truth, the whole truth and nothing but the truth. The truth, the whole truth and nothing but the truth,' he repeated. 'That's rather a lot to ask, my lord.'

'Mr Morgan, you must not talk like that.'

'But suppose I don't know the truth, my lord?'

'You must do your best.'

'That's all it means, is it, my lord? To do my best?'

'Of course.'

'Then why doesn't it say so?'

'Mr Stokes, will you kindly start your examination.'

'Is your name William Morgan and do you live at The Grange, Little Tempest, Sussex?'

'Quite so.'

'And are you a farmer?'

'Only in a small way.'

'Quite, but you do farm?'

'Not like my father.'

'Have you a farm?'

'I have a farm.'

'Right, let's get on,' said the judge. He was getting a little tired of William Morgan, service to his country notwithstanding.

'Have you found that there are a lot of official forms to fill in?' asked Stokes.

'Don't talk about them,' said Morgan.

'But we've got to. There's a lot of paperwork connected with farming?'

'I sometimes wonder if I've more paper on my farm than poultry.'

'And for some years did you try to do the paperwork yourself?'

'When it came to feeding the chicks or filling in the forms, I fed the chicks.'

'No doubt, but you did fill in forms?'

'Sometimes.'

'Did you read the forms before you filled them in?'

'Very rarely,' said Morgan.

'Did there come a time when proceedings were taken against you for making a false return?'

'There came several times.'

'And what happened?'

'I was fined. I refused to pay and went to prison. A good experience as a matter of fact. Everyone ought to do it. Well, perhaps not everyone,' he added as he looked at the judge.

The judge looked away from the witness.

'Are we coming to something relevant, Mr Stokes?' he asked.

'As soon as I can, my lord. Mr Morgan, did you meet anyone in prison?'

'A lot of people.'

'Anyone in particular?'

'The Governor, do you mean?'

'I do not. Did you meet a man called Wickham?'

'That's why I'm here now. I saw his name was mentioned in court.'

'It wasn't, you know.'

'I could have sworn it was.'

'Well, it wasn't.'

'Lucky I didn't swear it was.'

'Sometime or other, Mr Stokes,' began the judge, 'may the jury and I – '

'I'm sorry, my lord,' said Stokes. 'Well, Mr Morgan, what did this man Wickham say to you in prison?'

'He asked me if any of my friends cheated at cards.'

'And you said?'

'Of course.'

'Was that true?'

'Good gracious no, but he took me seriously.'

'What did he say?'

'He said that, if I could give him the names of one or two I'd seen cheat, he could help me to earn what he called an honest penny.'

'What did you say?'

'I asked him how it could be done. He said it was very simple. The sort of people I knew, he said, belonged to clubs and all that and they wouldn't want a scandal. So they'd pay to avoid it.'

'Well?'

'I decided to set a trap for this fellow as soon as I came out. And I got hold of a couple of friends and laid it all on. And one of them wrote a letter to the other pretending to apologise for what had happened. I took this to my prison friend and he was delighted, and said he'd introduce me to someone higher up the scale. And he introduced me to a man called Jones. Jones was very impressed when he heard the people I mixed with. I'm afraid I laid it on a bit thick. The things my friends did – cheating the Revenue, smuggling goods, bilking the railways – we were a fine lot I can tell you by the time I'd finished with us. Eventually Jones said he'd like me to meet his boss. And we made an appointment to meet this fellow and I met him.'

'Did you talk to him?'

'Indeed yes. He knew all about it. He was thick in it. He particularly liked income tax cases – false returns and all that. Because most people who cheated the Revenue had lots of money – that's one of the reasons they had it – and this chap reckoned that we were less thieves than the Revenue so that the money was better in our hands.'

'Would you recognise this man again?' asked Stokes.

'I think so.'

'Do you see him in court?'

'Where?'

'Anywhere. Look all round.'

Morgan looked round the court.

'You may leave the witness box, if you like,' said the judge.

'Thank you, my lord,' said Morgan and began to look at everyone in court. He was still enjoying himself immensely. He was the centre of attraction and he was going to make the most of it. After looking at the judge, the clerk, the jury and counsel he walked over to the dock and looked hard and long at Ledbury.

'That's him, my lord,' he said.

'Very well,' said the judge. 'You may return to the witness box.'

'Are you sure that is the man?' asked the judge.

'Yes, my lord,' said Morgan. 'That's the man.'

'Thank you, Mr Morgan,' said Stokes and sat down.

This is devilish awkward, thought Ledbury. I hadn't expected this. We've disposed of Margaret Vane but what can I do with this fellow? I think I know. He's too cocky by half. He thinks he's on a music-hall stage.

'Do you wish to cross-examine, Mr Ledbury?' asked the judge.

'Yes, please, my lord. Now, Mr Morgan, haven't you made a mistake?'

'A mistake?'

'Yes, a mistake. I do know of a man who's a little like me. I'm going to suggest to you that it was him you saw, not me. After all you had to come over here to look at me, didn't you?'

'That's true.'

'Now let me see if I can help you, Mr Morgan,' went on Ledbury. 'My face is smooth, isn't it, like yours?'

'Smooth?' queried Morgan. 'I don't understand.'

'Hadn't the man you saw got a nasty scar across his face as though he'd been gashed with a razor blade?'

Ledbury asked the question in such a way that the judge could not complain that he was threatening the witness. Yet the emphasis carried the threat across to Morgan, who suddenly understood.

'Gashed with a razor blade?' he repeated.

'That's right,' said Ledbury with as much menace as he dared. 'My face is untouched isn't it? Come and look, if you can't see from there. Would you like to? I'm sure his lordship would allow it again.'

'No, I can see from here.'

'What can you see, Mr Morgan?' asked Ledbury.

'Your face.'

'And you can see it hasn't been gashed. I repeat it's as smooth as your own.'

Morgan was no longer enjoying himself. He had come to Court full of enthusiasm and had loved every moment of it till then. But suddenly in a flash he realised that he was in a new and horrible world, a world he had read about not just in fiction but in the newspapers, a world full of gangsters who stopped at nothing, gangsters who slashed and killed. And he was being told in language he fully understood that, if he stayed in that world, he would be treated accordingly. He wished he had never been concerned in the case. Ledbury read his thoughts correctly and proceeded to adopt a sweetly persuasive, rather than a menacing approach.

'Are you sure you haven't made a mistake, Mr Morgan?' he asked. 'Hadn't the man you spoke to a big scar on his face?'

Morgan hesitated for a moment. Then he turned tail and fled.

'Yes, I think he had,' he said unhappily.

'Think a bit harder, Mr Morgan,' said Ledbury. 'Aren't you sure he had a scar? A nasty big scar, not a thing you'd be likely to forget.'

'Yes, he had a scar,' said Morgan.

'A big scar?' asked Ledbury.

'Yes, a big scar.'

'Quite sure now?'

'Yes, I'm quite sure.'

'I haven't a scar at all, have I?' asked Ledbury.

'No, you haven't.'

'Then it can't have been me you saw, can it, Mr Morgan?'

'No, I suppose not.'

'Suppose? I thought you were sure?'

'Yes, I'm sure.'

'Sure that it wasn't me?'

'Yes.'

'Thank you, Mr Morgan.'

Ledbury sat down, well pleased with his work. Stokes got up.

'Mr Morgan,' he said, 'it's quite plain that Mr Ledbury has no scar. How did you come to identify him at first?'

'I made a mistake,' said Morgan miserably. 'May I go now, please?'

Mr Stokes sat down with a sigh.

'Yes,' said the judge, 'you may go now.'

And William Morgan, who had come to court with such high hopes of being the belle of the ball with his picture in all the papers – 'Surprise witness' – interviews with the Press after the trial and so on and so forth – Mr Morgan walked miserably away, and devoutly hoped that his retraction had been sufficient to keep him from the attentions of Mr Ledbury's friends.

CHAPTER EIGHTEEN

Fear or Favour?

'Well, Mr Stokes,' said the judge when Morgan had gone, 'that doesn't carry us much further.'

'I'm afraid not, my lord,' said Stokes. 'I'll have Miss Vane recalled.'

Margaret came into court and went back into the witness box.

'Well, Miss Vane,' said the judge, 'what is the answer to my question? Were you employed by this man?'

There was no answer.

'You absolutely refuse to answer?' asked the judge.

'Yes, my lord.'

'My lord,' said Stokes, 'might I with respect know the relevance of the question?'

'Isn't it enough for you, Mr Stokes, that I have asked the question and she has refused to answer it and given no reason?'

'With respect, no, my lord. A question asked even by the judge must be relevant.'

'Are you teaching me the rules of evidence?'

'Oh, my lord, I wouldn't dream of – '

'Well – what are you doing then?'

'I am submitting on behalf of the prosecution that a witness should not be compelled to answer a question unless the question is material to the guilt or innocence of the accused.'

'How can you tell whether it's material?'

'Of course I can't, unless your lordship tells me. But, as your lordship knows, the prosecution can't appeal and there must be justice for the prosecution as well as the defence.'

'There you are again – justice,' said the judge.

'I hope I don't have to apologise for using that word in this court, my lord.'

The judge paused and stared in front of him.

'One day,' he said, 'you may be a judge yourself, Mr Stokes.'

'That's very good of your lordship.'

'I can only say that I hope you never have a decision of this kind to make.'

'Oh, my lord, I'm sure your lordship has had far more difficult matters to decide than this.'

'Are you? Let me think for a moment.'

After a short silence the judge looked at Margaret and said: 'Miss Vane – for the last time, do you positively refuse to answer my question?'

'I do, my lord.'

'Well, Mr Stokes,' said the judge, 'can you carry the matter any further?'

'Not with this witness, my lord.'

'But can you proceed with the case?'

'With the case? Certainly, my lord.'

'Have you any other evidence?'

'No, my lord.'

'So that is the case for the prosecution?'

'Subject to any further questions of the witness.'

'Have you any further questions, Mr Ledbury?'

'No, my lord,' said Ledbury.

'Have you, Mr Stokes?'

'Miss Vane, have you any doubt that it was the accused with whom you discussed the blackmail cases in the park?'

'That is a leading question, Mr Stokes,' said the judge.

'She's already said it, my lord.'

'Then there's no need to ask her again. What you were seeking to do was to add emphasis to her previous answers, but the emphasis comes from you and not from her.'

'I'm sorry, my lord. Thank you, Miss Vane.'

'I shall consider your position later, Miss Vane,' said the judge. 'You may leave the box. Well now, Mr Stokes,' he went on, 'would you ask the jury to convict on this evidence?'

'There is evidence to go before them.'

'Of course there's evidence, but your vital witness has refused to answer a perfectly simple question and has given no reason whatever for her refusal. How can the jury rely on such a witness?'

'That is a matter for them when they've heard the whole case.'

'They may think they've heard enough already.' The judge looked towards the jury box.

'Might I address the jury, my lord?' asked Stokes.

'Not unless they want the case to proceed. Do you wish to hear any more, members of the jury? If you want to discuss the matter, pray do.'

After a few minutes' discussion in the jury box, the man on the right stood up.

'Are you agreed about the matter, Mr Foreman?' asked the judge.

'Yes, my lord.'

'You have heard enough, you mean?' said the judge.

'Yes, my lord.'

'Put the question, please, Mr Anthony,' said the judge, looking down to the clerk.

'Members of the jury, are you agreed upon your verdict?' asked the clerk.

'We are, my lord.'

'Do you find the prisoner Clifton Ledbury not guilty?'

'We do, my lord.'

'Not guilty and that is the verdict of you all?'

'Yes, my lord.'

'Very well, then. Thank you for your help, members of the jury.'

The judge rose. 'I shall not sit again until this afternoon,' he said and left the court.

'What about me?' said Ledbury.

CHAPTER NINETEEN

No Fear or Favour

'Let him out, officer,' said the clerk, and one of the officers opened the door of the dock.

'Be a good chap,' said Ledbury, 'and fetch me my hat and coat. They're downstairs.'

Gradually the court cleared. As Stokes went out with the Director he said: 'I simply don't understand it. What on earth can have come over him? It's the most astonishing performance I've ever seen.'

Everyone except the superintendent had left the court when Ledbury's hat and coat arrived. He thanked the officer, came out of the dock and walked up to the superintendent. He walked slowly, in the way that a person who wants to run as fast as he can sometimes does.

'No hard feelings, superintendent?' he said.

'None sir. One can't win every case. P'raps we'll get you next time.'

'But there won't be a next time.'

'Going abroad?'

'Could be.'

'Why d'you say there won't be a next time? Closing down?'

'You could say that.'

'Bit dangerous to say that to me, isn't it?' asked the superintendent.

'Dangerous? Why? I've been acquitted. I could tell you I'd done it and there's nothing you could do about it.'

'That's true enough,' said the superintendent.

'You couldn't even get me for perjury. I never gave evidence.'

'Too true.'

'So I could tell you it *was* me quite safely.'

'But you wouldn't dare do that.'

'Don't you believe it. All right. It was me. The girl was telling the truth.'

'You don't say?' said the superintendent.

'I do say. Don't you believe me?'

'Oh yes, I believe you.'

'And what are you going to do about it?'

'What *can* I do?'

'Nothing.'

'A pity but there it is,' said the superintendent. 'I must say you put up a wonderful fight. You had the old judge eating out of your hand in the end.'

'He did a bit, didn't he? But I thought he was going to turn awkward once or twice.'

'Funny the way he couldn't make up his mind – that's not like him.'

'I wouldn't know.'

'It was as though there was some sort of outside pressure on him. That's how it seemed to me. You weren't hypnotising him, I suppose?'

'Not my line,' said Ledbury.

'But didn't you feel sometimes that he behaved as though someone had a hand on his shoulder?' asked the superintendent.

'Not that I noticed. He was just like a flipping judge to me.'

'You've not been in front of one before?'

'Oh dear no. Just what I've read.'

'About friends of yours?'

'About people. I've picked up a bit about the law, you know.'

'I must say I was surprised that we ever got on to you at all.'

'Well, you shouldn't have.'

'You've got to hand it to that girl.'

'I'd hand it to her all right, if I had the chance.'

'I wonder why she wouldn't answer that one question.'

Ledbury laughed.

'You don't know, do you?' asked the superintendent.

'As a matter of fact, I do.'

'Tell me.'

'What'll you tell me in return?'

'What d'you want to know?'

'Who cracked first – Jones or Nottingham?'

'All right. I'll tell you, if you'll tell me.'

'OK. You go first.'

'No – you.'

'We'll toss for it,' said Ledbury.

The superintendent tossed a coin. 'Call', he said.

'Heads. It is. Which one was it?'

'What does it matter? They're both dead.'

'Are you suggesting – '

'I'm not suggesting anything. They're dead and you know it.'

'I don't know anything of the sort.'

'You do, because I've told you. It was Nottingham. Now it's my turn. Why wouldn't she answer the question?'

'Well – I'm only guessing, mind you.'

'Oh – come. You said you knew. Why wouldn't she answer?'

'Well – I couldn't tell for certain, could I? I never saw what the judge wrote down.'

'That's true. What do you think it was?'

'A name.'

'Of course it was a name, but whose?'

'That girl was in the secret service,' said Ledbury. 'And the name the old man wrote down was one she could never admit to knowing.'

'But how could the judge have known it? Where did he get it from?'

'A friendly hint, I expect.'

'From your brother?'

'Shouldn't be surprised.'

'D'you think your brother gave him any other hints?'

'How should I know? I've been in prison all the time.'

'But you saw your brother in Brixton. He may have told you.'

'Not while I was inside. I might have talked in my sleep. I must say you've taken this very well. Doesn't a case like this interfere with your promotion?'

'Good gracious no. One can only do one's best. After all, I couldn't tell the judge what to do. And, if he tells the jury to acquit, that's not my fault.'

'But shouldn't you have known about the secret service? After all, she was your witness.'

'I don't know. Perhaps. But I can believe she was in the secret service. It needs courage and she'd plenty of that. And that would account for her squeezing herself into your organisation. A pretty dangerous assignment.'

'I can agree with you there. It's always been dangerous to interfere with me.'

'D'you think the judge was frightened of you?'

'I suppose he might have been frightened that one of my representatives might come along.'

'D'you think one did?'

'Well – I wouldn't be telling you if he had, would I? You could still get me for that. So for the benefit of the record let me say here and now that I was not party to any threat which may or may not have been made to the judge.'

'Well, that's all right then,' said the superintendent. 'That clears the air.'

At that moment a policeman came in, whispered to the superintendent and then went out again.

'Next job?' queried Ledbury.

'It wasn't, as a matter of fact. Winding up the present one.'

'You have to make a report, I suppose, explaining why I was acquitted.'

'Something like that.'

'Well – I really must be going now. It's been nice knowing you.'

'Just one moment. I want to tell you something,' said the superintendent. 'Your friends certainly keep their word.'

'What's that?'

'She's back.'

'Who's back?'

'Don't you know?'

'No idea.'

'Someone's daughter.'

'Well, every woman's that. D'you mean Margaret Vane?'

'I mean Angela Hereford.'

'Who's she?'

'The judge's daughter.'

'So he had a daughter. Why should that interest me?'

'She's back. She was kidnapped, you know.'

'No! How terrible,' said Ledbury.

'They promised her back as soon as you'd been acquitted.'

'So that's why you said we keep our word.'

'I didn't say you – I said your friends kept their word – but if you're in it too, I'd be happy to give you the credit as well.'

'I don't know anything about it,' said Ledbury.

'Why did you say "*we* keep our word" then?' asked the superintendent.

'It was a slip.'

'If only you'd make a few more.'

'Well – I shan't. Goodbye, superintendent.'

'Please don't go yet.'

'I'm sorry. I must.'

'Then I must put it more forcibly. You're not to go.'

'You can't hold me.'

'Oh yes, I can.'

'We'll see about that.'

He strode to the door. Two policemen barred his way. 'What is this?' he complained. 'Are you charging me with something else? Just because I said "we keep our word".'

'That wasn't enough.'

'Well – let me go then.'

'I'm afraid not.'

'What are you keeping me for?'

'Your trial.'

'My trial for what?'

'Didn't *you* listen? Conspiracy to blackmail.'

'Didn't you listen? I've been acquitted.'

'You haven't, you know.'

'Look, I'm not finding this very funny,' said Ledbury.

'It's not meant to be funny.'

'Were you in court when the jury gave their verdict?'

'No, I wasn't,' said the superintendent.

'Well – ask someone who was. They'll tell you I was found not guilty. But I saw you sitting there.'

'Quite right, I was.'

'But you said you weren't in court when the jury gave its verdict.'

'Right again. I wasn't.'

Ledbury went to the door again. Again his way was barred.

'Will you kindly explain? What are you keeping me for?'

'I told you. Your trial.'

'But it's over. Once I've been acquitted I'm free forever. That's the law, isn't it?'

'Yes, that's the law.'

'Then what are you playing at?'

'You haven't been acquitted.'

'You *were* in court. The foreman said not guilty. Didn't you hear him?'

'No.'

'I can't help it if you're deaf.'

'I'm not. I heard everything that was said.'

'Is this a joke?'

'I told you it wasn't.'

'Well, I warn you. I'll sue for false imprisonment.'

'You'll fail.'

At that moment the judge came in and sat down.

'Thank God,' said Ledbury. 'My lord, he won't let me go. Will you order him to do so, please.'

'I'm afraid not.'

'But, once a man's been acquitted, he's free forever, isn't he? Whatever other evidence may turn up. That's the law, isn't it?'

'Yes,' said the judge, 'that's the law. But you haven't been acquitted.'

'But I've been acquitted. The foreman said so.'

'The foreman wasn't in Court. The man who said "not guilty" was a policeman. He was substituted for the foreman.'

'Substituted? Rubbish. It was the same man.'

'He *looked* the same,' said the judge. 'The superintendent chose someone of the same general appearance as the foreman and he wore similar clothes. Don't forget, you'd only seen the foreman for three-quarters of an hour on Friday. Every precaution was taken to prevent your noticing the change.'

'How do I know you're not kidding?'

'Bring them in, superintendent,' said the judge.

'If this is true, it's monstrous,' said Ledbury.

'Not as monstrous as killing a little girl would have been,' said the judge.

The superintendent came in with a man.

'This is the real foreman, my lord,' he said.

'Now the other,' said the judge.

The superintendent opened the door and beckoned, and another man came in.

'This is Constable Hughes, my lord,' said the superintendent.

'Take a good look at him, Mr Ledbury,' said the judge. 'This is the man who said "not guilty".'

'It's a fraud.'

'I suppose it is in a way,' said the judge. 'But just think. My daughter had to be saved and you had to be given a fair trial. Can you think of any other way by which it could be done? At any rate neither the Lord Chancellor nor the Attorney-General with whom I discussed the matter over the weekend could think of any alternative. While you're awaiting your trial, Mr Ledbury, perhaps you'll see if you can hit on a better solution.'

'But the people in that box said I was not guilty and once that's done I'm free.'

'The only people who could lawfully pronounce you not guilty were the jurymen who were sworn to try you. And one of them wasn't there.'

'But we have majority verdicts now,' said Ledbury. 'It was eleven to one.'

'It wasn't anything of the sort,' said the judge. 'To give a valid verdict it must be the verdict, whether unanimous or by a majority, of the whole jury. One of them wasn't present on the second day. From 10.30 this morning your trial became a mock trial, Mr Ledbury.'

'Then you were just play-acting,' said Ledbury. 'And the jury too.'

'Eleven of the jury and one policeman, yes. Your brother warned me that it ought to appear to be genuine. He told me to act as I've never acted before. And I certainly did.'

'You can't get away with this. I shall appeal.'

'But, Mr Ledbury, until you've been tried and convicted, you can't appeal. You will now remain in custody until the publicity of the case has blown over. And you will then be tried by a fresh jury before a fresh judge. And I should warn you and your associates that that judge will probably be a bachelor and will have a permanent guard over him before it is announced that he is to try the case. The fresh jury will be similarly guarded. And in case you have other ideas for yourself – so will you.'

'But I've admitted my guilt now as a result of all this,' said Ledbury desperately.

'Has he, superintendent?' asked the judge.

'He has indeed, my lord.'

'Well,' said the judge, 'that may simplify the task of the new jury.'

And, as he left the court, Mr Justice Hereford permitted himself the suspicion of a smile.

Henry Cecil

According to the Evidence

Alec Morland is on trial for murder. He has tried to remedy the ineffectiveness of the law by taking matters into his own hands. Unfortunately for him, his alleged crime was not committed in immediate defence of others or of himself. In this fascinating murder trial you will not find out until the very end just how the law will interpret his actions. Will his defence be accepted or does a different fate await him?

The Asking Price

Ronald Holbrook is a fifty-seven-year-old bachelor who has lived in the same house for twenty years. Jane Doughty, the daughter of his next-door neighbours, is seventeen. She suddenly decides she is in love with Ronald and wants to marry him. Everyone is amused at first but then events take a disturbingly sinister turn and Ronald finds himself enmeshed in a potentially tragic situation.

'The secret of Mr Cecil's success lies in continuing to do superbly what everyone now knows he can do well.'
The Sunday Times

HENRY CECIL

BRIEF TALES FROM THE BENCH

What does it feel like to be a Judge? Read these stories and you can almost feel you are looking at proceedings from the lofty position of the Bench.

With a collection of eccentric and amusing characters, Henry Cecil brings to life the trials in a County Court and exposes the complex and often contradictory workings of the English legal system.

'Immensely readable. His stories rely above all on one quality – an extraordinary, an arresting, a really staggering ingenuity.'
New Statesman

BROTHERS IN LAW

Roger Thursby, aged twenty-four, is called to the bar. He is young, inexperienced and his love life is complicated. He blunders his way through a succession of comic adventures including his calamitous debut at the bar.

His career takes an upward turn when he is chosen to defend the caddish Alfred Green at the Old Bailey. In this first Roger Thursby novel Henry Cecil satirizes the legal profession with his usual wit and insight.

'Uproariously funny.' *The Times*

'Full of charm and humour. I think it is the best Henry Cecil yet.' P G Wodehouse

HENRY CECIL

HUNT THE SLIPPER

Harriet and Graham have been happily married for twenty years. One day Graham fails to return home and Harriet begins to realise she has been abandoned. This feeling is strengthened when she starts to receive monthly payments from an untraceable source. After five years on her own Harriet begins to see another man and divorces Graham on the grounds of his desertion. Then one evening Harriet returns home to find Graham sitting in a chair, casually reading a book. Her initial relief turns to anger and then to fear when she realises that if Graham's story is true, she may never trust his sanity again. This complex comedy thriller will grip your attention to the very last page.

SOBER AS A JUDGE

Roger Thursby, the hero of *Brothers in Law* and *Friends at Court*, continues his career as a High Court judge. He presides over a series of unusual cases, including a professional debtor and an action about a consignment of oranges which turned to juice before delivery. There is a delightful succession of eccentric witnesses as the reader views proceedings from the Bench.

'The author's gift for brilliant characterisation makes this a book that will delight lawyers and laymen as much as did its predecessors.' *The Daily Telegraph*

OTHER TITLES BY HENRY CECIL AVAILABLE DIRECT
FROM HOUSE OF STRATUS

Quantity		£	$(US)	$(CAN)	€
	ACCORDING TO THE EVIDENCE	6.99	11.50	15.99	11.50
	ALIBI FOR A JUDGE	6.99	11.50	15.99	11.50
	THE ASKING PRICE	6.99	11.50	15.99	11.50
	BRIEF TALES FROM THE BENCH	6.99	11.50	15.99	11.50
	BROTHERS IN LAW	6.99	11.50	15.99	11.50
	THE BUTTERCUP SPELL	6.99	11.50	15.99	11.50
	CROSS PURPOSES	6.99	11.50	15.99	11.50
	DAUGHTERS IN LAW	6.99	11.50	15.99	11.50
	FATHERS IN LAW	6.99	11.50	15.99	11.50
	FRIENDS AT COURT	6.99	11.50	15.99	11.50
	FULL CIRCLE	6.99	11.50	15.99	11.50
	HUNT THE SLIPPER	6.99	11.50	15.99	11.50
	INDEPENDENT WITNESS	6.99	11.50	15.99	11.50

ALL HOUSE OF STRATUS BOOKS ARE AVAILABLE FROM GOOD BOOKSHOPS OR
DIRECT FROM THE PUBLISHER:

Internet: **www.houseofstratus.com** including author interviews, reviews, features.

Email: **sales@houseofstratus.com** please quote author, title and credit card details.

OTHER TITLES BY HENRY CECIL AVAILABLE DIRECT
FROM HOUSE OF STRATUS

Quantity		£	$(US)	$(CAN)	€
	MUCH IN EVIDENCE	6.99	11.50	15.99	11.50
	NATURAL CAUSES	6.99	11.50	15.99	11.50
	NO BAIL FOR THE JUDGE	6.99	11.50	15.99	11.50
	THE PAINSWICK LINE	6.99	11.50	15.99	11.50
	PORTRAIT OF A JUDGE	6.99	11.50	15.99	11.50
	SETTLED OUT OF COURT	6.99	11.50	15.99	11.50
	SOBER AS A JUDGE	6.99	11.50	15.99	11.50
	TELL YOU WHAT I'LL DO	6.99	11.50	15.99	11.50
	TRUTH WITH HER BOOTS ON	6.99	11.50	15.99	11.50
	UNLAWFUL OCCASIONS	6.99	11.50	15.99	11.50
	THE WANTED MAN	6.99	11.50	15.99	11.50
	WAYS AND MEANS	6.99	11.50	15.99	11.50
	A WOMAN NAMED ANNE	6.99	11.50	15.99	11.50

ALL HOUSE OF STRATUS BOOKS ARE AVAILABLE FROM GOOD BOOKSHOPS OR
DIRECT FROM THE PUBLISHER:

Hotline: UK ONLY: **0800 169 1780**, please quote author, title and credit card
details.
INTERNATIONAL: **+44 (0) 20 7494 6400**, please quote author, title,
and credit card details.

Send to: **House of Stratus**
24c Old Burlington Street
London
W1X 1RL
UK

Please allow following carriage costs per ORDER
(For goods up to free carriage limits shown)

	£(Sterling)	$(US)	$(CAN).	€(Euros)
UK	1.95	3.20	4.29	3.00
Europe	2.95	4.99	6.49	5.00
North America	2.95	4.99	6.49	5.00
Rest of World	2.95	5.99	7.75	6.00
Free carriage for goods value over:	50	75	100	75

PLEASE SEND CHEQUE, POSTAL ORDER (STERLING ONLY), EUROCHEQUE, OR INTERNATIONAL MONEY ORDER (PLEASE CIRCLE METHOD OF PAYMENT YOU WISH TO USE) MAKE PAYABLE TO: STRATUS HOLDINGS plc

Order total including postage:_____Please tick currency you wish to use and add total amount of order:

☐ £ (Sterling) ☐ $ (US) ☐ $ (CAN) ☐ € (EUROS)

VISA, MASTERCARD, SWITCH, AMEX, SOLO, JCB:

☐☐☐☐☐☐☐☐☐☐☐☐☐☐☐☐☐☐☐☐☐☐☐☐

Issue number (Switch only):

☐☐☐

Start Date:

☐☐ / ☐☐

Expiry Date:

☐☐ / ☐☐

Signature: _____

NAME: _____

ADDRESS: _____

_____

_____

POSTCODE: _____

Please allow 28 days for delivery.

Prices subject to change without notice.
Please tick box if you do not wish to receive any additional information. ☐

House of Stratus publishes many other titles in this genre; please check our website (**www.houseofstratus.com**) for more details